Books of Merit

The Secret Language of Girls

Josey Vogels

The Secret Language of Girls

Thomas Allen Publishers
Toronto

National Library of Canada Cataloguing in Publication Data

Vogels, Josey
    The secret language of girls

Includes bibliographical references.
ISBN 0-88762-102-3

1. Girls.   I. Title.

HQ1233.V63 2002   305.4   C2001-904266-3

Cover design: La Liberté
Text design: Gordon Robertson
Editor: Katja Pantzar
Copy-editor: Alison Reid
Author photograph on cover: Tshi

Published by Thomas Allen Publishers,
a division of Thomas Allen & Son Limited,
145 Front Street East, Suite 209,
Toronto, Ontario M5A 1E3 Canada

Printed and bound in Canada

Acknowledgements

So many people supported me in the writing of this book.

A huge thank you goes to my editrix extraordinaire, Katja Pantzar, whose constant patience, encouragement, feedback, and belief in the project kept me going. Thanks to all the folks at Thomas Allen Publishers, especially Patrick, Denise, and Gord, who have welcomed me with open arms and done everything to make this one of the most pleasant book publishing experiences I've had.

Thank you to Denise, my agent, who found these fabulous folks for me. Thanks also to my brilliant researchers, Adrienne Shiffman and Zeina Awad. A big, wet thank you to my ever lovely assistant, Karen LaRocca, for holding up the fort while I was busy writing, for doing research, reading rough drafts and buying me a nude thong (don't ask).

A monster thank you goes to my Monkey, the love of my life and the pillar on which all of this leans.

Thanks also to Matt, Tara, and Katia. I love you guys so much and working with you on the TV show was one of the most satisfying experiences of my life. Thank you for your insight, encouragement, and feedback on this project. And for Banff.

I owe a ton of thanks to all the women who shared their stories and insights for this book.

Thanks to my mom, who taught me early on about the strength of women, and to my sisters for their awesome support and those hilarious girls' nights.

And finally, of course, I have to thank the women with whom I share the Secret Language of Girls every day— my girlfriends Audrey, Wanda, Linda, Li, Darcelle, Char, Jenny, Ilana, Sarah, Jillian, Isabel, Buffy, and the many more I don't have room to mention here. Thanks for your feedback, your unwavering belief in me, and the endless girl fun. I love you all dearly.

Contents

Introduction

Be she old, or be she young,
A woman's strength is in her tongue.
— WELSH SAYING

Can I Let You in on a Secret?

You are very rich in good, strong female friends who I know will always be there for you. It is such a comfort for me to know that you have experienced the support and love that can only come from women. It will see you through anything.

A dear friend of mine whose mother recently died of breast cancer read this passage as part of her mom's eulogy. It was from a letter her mother had written to her while she was in university.

I was one of the good, strong friends her mother referred to in the letter. I still am. We don't see each other as much as we did in university when "chick nights" were a regular excuse to get into all kinds of trouble. But we still see each other through everything.

I love the company of women. In an era when family is often scattered or far away and life moves us from place to place, my female friends are the closest thing to "home" that I have. When I am with close female friends, I don't have to explain things or make excuses or try to impress them. I can kick my feet up, knowing they will compliment my footwear, and I can bask in the joy of being in a world that I understand.

And while I don't necessarily believe that men and women are from different planets, I do often feel as if men and women grow up in different worlds, each with our own language, or at the very least, vocabulary. Kind of like how Brits put things in the "boot" of their car while we North Americans put them in the "trunk." We're all speaking English, but words have different meanings. In male and female language, the word "boot" also means different things. For guys, boots are things they wear so their feet don't get wet. For women, boots are something we go off in search of like the Holy Grail and we don't stop until we find the perfect pair, with the perfect heel and the perfectly squared off toe that make the perfect statement about us. Of course, by the time we find them, pointy boots have come back into style and the quest begins again.

The language that women speak never struck me as secret or mysterious, but I guess that's because I grew up speaking it. I take it for granted. It doesn't seem to me anything but perfectly natural for a girlfriend to call me long distance and find me watching the Miss America Beauty Pageant and immediately tune in to the same channel so we can settle in and watch it together, joking and laughing over the phone at the absurdity of it all one minute and admiring a contestant's outfit the next. Turns out guys don't do this kind of stuff. Go figure.

In fact, I realized that guys don't get a lot of what women do or say. That's when it struck me that maybe there was a Secret Language that women shared. Once I got this in my head, I couldn't let it go. Suddenly, I saw evidence of the Secret Language of Girls, or SLOG—as it affectionately came to be referred to while I was writing this book—everywhere.

Whether I was immersed in a heart-to-heart with a best friend over her love life, her career, or what she should wear to an art opening that she knew an ex who broke her heart was also going to be attending, or found myself surrounded by a room of shrieking, laughing half-naked women knee-deep in a pile of clothing at a switch-and-bitch session, I realized I had taken the communication and rituals I share with women for granted.

I had never really sat down and thought about how it is that women have developed the intricate web of vocabulary, rituals and experiences that we all recognize as female communication.

Was it genetic? Did we learn it? Was it something in the water?

I decided I needed to get to the bottom of it.

I talked to tons of women, I read books and interviewed people who study how women communicate at various stages in their lives. What I discovered was that the Secret Language, like most languages, has deep historical roots. Women, it turns out, have been sharing and yakking for ages. Long excluded from male society, we hung out with the girls and developed our own culture. And whether that was gathering around a quilt or a new mother, much of our culture revolved around talking to each other.

In fact, it has long been felt that women talk too much. Our "chatter" has long been dismissed as gossip. Some of us were even burned at the stake for our "slippery tongues." Obviously, the boys weren't keen on all our yammering. Not that this stopped us from talking.

The Secret Language of Girls has carried on through generations. Mothers pass it on to daughters and young girls learn it from the moment they learn to turn a skipping rope in the schoolyard.

We talk each other through puberty and the discovery of boys. After all, only another woman can truly understand what it's like when we first get our periods or how much it means to have the right hair in high school. Only a woman can understand and appreciate the joy of laughing with another woman until you cry, of knowing exactly what the other person means without having to speak at all, of having someone know you inside out and of being understood.

Another woman understands the excitement of finding out that your favourite shoe store is having a two-for-one sale. And why, yes, we always need another pair of shoes.

I talk about how female styles of communication help and hinder us in the workplace. Is women's language really as powerless as we are often led to believe? And how life changes—work, relationships, marriage, kids, divorce—can both threaten and strengthen our Secret Language. (Why do you think we invented girls' weekends?)

I realize too that female bonding isn't all girly drinks and late-night powwows over boys, life, and clothes. Female bonding and communication also has its troubles. I address how our need to feel connected to other women can sometimes be overshadowed by feelings of competition and envy.

I talk about how the Secret Language grows old with us and matures, only getting better with age.

And finally, for the uninitiated, I've included a beginner's guide to the Secret Language—a sort of glossary of what we say versus what we mean. (Girls, you might wanna leave the book lying around the john, open to this section.)

The Secret Language of Girls explains female bonding and "girl" culture. It explores the history, the myths, and the rituals that bind us from childhood through adolescence and into adulthood.

It explores where our need to connect comes from, whether it's because our brains are wired differently, or because we bleed every month, or because we are biologically or socially programmed to think of others first.

Being female is a unique and wonderful experience. And the Language we share throughout our lives is one that I savour.

In fact, the Secret Language goes perfectly with a bottle of Beaujolais. So why not pour yourself a glass and curl up with *The Secret Language of Girls*? I'm sure you'll enjoy the company.

From
the Mouths
of Babes

Words are women's tools.

— HELEN E. FISHER, The First Sex: The Natural Talents of
Women and How They Are Changing the World

Where Did You Get
That Fabulous Loincloth?

When was the last time you had the boys over for a good old chinwag? Didn't think so. Boys just don't seem to need to talk the way we girls do. I'd like to say it wasn't always this way. Actually, I take that back. I'm quite proud to say it has always been this way.

The Secret Language of Girls is an ancient language that has existed as long as women have. I can just imagine the gals kicking back at the cave, munching on a bowl of seeds and berries, admiring each other's loincloth.

"Where did you get that cute little number? I've never seen one made from wildebeest before."

"Thanks, isn't it great? That lovely cavewoman down the road—you know the one with those cute drawings all over her cave—gave it to me. Said she never wears it."

But women don't just need to talk in order to gush over each other's outfits and confuse men (as fun as that may be); talking to other woman has long been essential for our basic survival.

"Words are women's tools," Helen E. Fisher, anthropologist and author of *The First Sex* tells me over the phone from her New York office. "Women have used words for millions of years to connect to others, to give support to others, to conduct their love affairs and to raise their young. Words are real intimacy to women." In *The First Sex*, Fisher describes the evolution of the male thought process, something she calls "step thinking," and female thought, which she calls "web thinking."

"A million years ago, ancestral men were building fires, chipping stone hand axes, and hunting big animals in East Africa—concentration and focus were required for such tasks —those who didn't pay attention were trampled on, gored, or eaten." Ancestral women, on the other hand, worked at raising long-dependent children under highly dangerous conditions. This required some serious multi-tasking, tremendous communication, and support-network-building skills.

According to Fisher, "In order to rear helpless infants, ancestral mothers needed to do a lot of things at the same time. Watch for snakes. Listen for thunder. Taste for poison. Rock the sleepy. Distract the cranky. Instruct the curious. Soothe the fearful. Inspire the tardy. Feed the hungry. Mothers had to do countless daily chores while they stoked the fire, cooked the food, and talked to friends."

Obviously, a lot can change in a million years, and Fisher acknowledges that while being gored or trampled doesn't pose quite the threat it once did, we carry this luggage from the past into the present. Just look at the Internet, the most modern communication forum around. Susan Herring, an associate professor of Information Science at the University of California at Berkeley, conducted a study on how women communicate online. Herring tells me she studied communication styles in chat rooms and found that in all-female chats, "there were more overt expressions of politeness, thanks, and appreciation, as well as expressions of support of others." In other words, women were busy building connections.

In chats where men participated, the differences in our communication styles really shone, she says. "The adult females were more likely to agree or present themselves as being aligned with other women in the group, whereas men were more likely to take an oppositional stance." In a heated argument online, women withdrew and were reluctant to participate—they would say things like "I felt intimidated," or "I didn't want to say anything because I thought I would be attacked."

Interestingly, when Herring tried to turn the tables and use a more "male" style of communication for a few days in an online chat group on linguistics—that is, being blunt and direct—she found that females got mad.

"With all-female groups," Herring tells me, "you tend to get a more egalitarian strategy; women overlap [with] other women—they tend not to interrupt but rather overlap supportively."

I know exactly what you mean, Ms. Herring, and so sorry to butt in like this but I just want to give a little bit of background here. Do you mind?

Oh, please, Josey, go right ahead.

A Slip of the Tongue

So women communicate differently from men. No big secret there, right? We've all been to dinner parties only to find that by the end of the night, a gaggle of women are whooping it up on one side of the room—sharing, dishing, and probably talking about sex—while a knot of men busy themselves on the other side of the room talking about . . . um, well, okay, that's another book.

But how did this come to be? How is it that two women who meet for the first time can find themselves engrossed in a deep conversation about life, politics, infidelity, men, where they bought their fabulous shoes, and whether they go battery or plug-in? And why all the furtiveness?

I could use that famous old trick and blame it all on Eve. In her essay in *A History of Women in the West: Silences of the Middle Ages*, French medieval historian and literature professor Danielle Régnier-Bohler says some folks (read *men*) believed that if we ladies weren't such "interminable chatterers," Eve would have been listening better. She would have realized that the Devil's "sweet veiled words" were actually a big smarmy come-on and saved us all a lot of trouble.

Eve isn't the only woman to take flak for being a chatterbox, though I can't imagine whom she chattered with (girls' night would be a bit of a bust if you're the only chick around). If women have needed to talk since our first girls' night back at the cave, men have been trying to get us to shut up for just as long.

"In the medieval West, women talked. They talked a great deal. Men felt that they talked too much, and 'chatter' was among the foremost of the faults of women denounced by preachers," writes French medieval historian Georges Duby in *A History of Women in the West*.

Truth be told, talk show hosts like Oprah or Jerry Springer wouldn't have stood a chance back in medieval times. Back then, people weren't big on talk in general, writes Duby, as they considered "all language to be a trap." It was believed that women were inherently deceptive, that we were talking about the boys behind their backs, and that we were having way too much fun (you'll probably find a few supporters of these theories even today). But my favourite explanation for why men found women to be such annoying chatterboxes has to be the slippery tongue theory, as explained by British medieval historian Henrietta Leyser in her book *Medieval Women: A Social History of Women in England 450-1500.*

Using a complex formula based on the Greek Hippocratic theory, folks back in the Middle Ages divided the world into four elements: fire, air, earth, and water. By measuring a person's body temperature, their level of body moisture, and the colour of their bile, they determined that men were hotter and drier than women, which accounted for men's physiological and moral superiority (and may explain why some men are so full of hot air). Women were considered wet and cold, and this apparently accounted for both their physical weaknesses, untrustworthy natures, and for their slippery tongues.

"'Women's tongues' are the ready butt of medieval misogyny," writes Leyser. "It was something of a commonplace that women were garrulous and talked more than men because their bodies were wetter, so their tongues slipped around more easily in their mouths."

What a load of horses—t. Sorry, that just, uh, slipped out. I should probably hold my tongue.

This theory would be quite laughable if it didn't get us into so much trouble. Thanks to wonky thinking like this, thousands of slippery-tongued women were tried, convicted, and tortured during the witch hunts of the Middle Ages. Some women, many of whom were not witches at all, were even permanently silenced just for being "the more talkative sex."

According to *The Malleus Maleficarum* (The Witch Hammer), a 1486 guidebook published to aid witch hunters in the identification, prosecution, and dispatching of witches, chattiness alone made women a target: "As for . . . why a greater number of witches is found in the fragile feminine sex than among men . . . the first reason is that they are more credulous, and since the chief aim of the devil is to corrupt faith, therefore he rather attacks them . . . the second reason is that women are naturally more impressionable . . . the third reason is that they have slippery tongues and are unable to conceal from their fellow-women those things which by evil arts they know."

Who knew swapping a few spells or your mom's apple pie recipe would send the boys into such a panic? It's no wonder we ladies took our language underground where we could enjoy it without male interference. It was either that or turning them all into toads.

It's still hard to understand why the boys were so down on our constant chatting. I know it might get a little annoying once in a while, say when you're trying to read the newspaper or watch the game, but it hardly warrants being burned at the stake. And how did it evolve to the point that today when guys get together they "swap stories" and "shoot the shit" while women have "hen parties," "chin wags," or "bitch sessions" where we yak, gab, chatter, natter, prattle, nag, bitch, whine, and gossip? I mean it's just girl talk. Why all the negativity?

Karma Lochrie believes that men belittled women's talk out of fear. In her book, *Covert Operations: The Medieval Uses of Secrecy*, the professor of English at Indiana University explores how women's gossip shaped attitudes about secrecy in the Middle Ages. "Just as women's bodies and sexuality were commonly associated with secrecy (and deception) . . . so their speech was conceived as occult and transgressive," she writes. Women's talk was considered messy and indiscreet, she explains. Of course, the biggest fear among the boys was that we were revealing secrets about them. "Women's gossip consists of men's secrets exchanged, and worse, enlarged upon and proliferated by women's indiscreet speech," writes Lochrie.

Really now. So sensitive, these boys. He thinks if we tell our girlfriends that he cries during beer ads, the world as we know it will crumble. And it figures. Just like the boys to think it's all about them. We do talk about other things, you know. No really, we do.

Oral Pleasures

Gossip (which I'll happily be indulging in later on in the book) was one of the most despised forms of verbal exchange among women. I swear, you'd think we were implementing mandatory shopping days for men, given all the fear and loathing it induced.

In the Middle Ages, gossip was considered a vice, according to Lochrie, and women were the ones most often in its grip. What was troubling was that gossip made personal affairs public and didn't respect silly things like academic and scientific proof. The fact that women could delight in the sheer superficiality of gossip with blatant disregard for male institutions and authority seriously bugged the boys. So much so that while we may associate gossip with the stuff of tabloids and rumour, the Middle Ages assigned gossip a place among the Seven Deadly Sins and believed it to be a female vice of extraordinary power.

Perhaps this explains the sinful pleasure one derives from gossiping. But we can't have the girls pleasuring themselves now, can we? According to Lochrie, gossip was also feared because it was seen as a voyeuristic, even erotic pleasure. Even back then, they knew it really all came down to sex. Because we all know that's what makes for the really good gossip.

Danielle Régnier-Bohler talks about how women bond through gossip not just because the activity is taboo but also because, often, so is the subject matter. "Linguistic taboos in general are closely intertwined with sexual taboos," she writes. "Casually uttering forbidden words, laughing over them, and punning on them helped bind women together as a group. At times this ribald talk amounted to something like a rite of initiation."

And a hell of a lot of fun. Too much fun for some people's tastes. The attitude that linked women's talk to sinful plea-sure persisted long past the Middle Ages. Folks felt this "self-indulgent gadding" preoccupied with "sexual conduct and scandal" fed into a rising problem of "loose talk and lax sexual behaviour among women," according to Melanie Tebbutt Aldershot in *Women's Talk? A Social History of "Gossip" in*

Working-Class Neighbourhoods: 1880-1960. "Women's language became linked with wandering verbally and sexually."

Heaven forbid you go off gadding with friends and neighbours, because if you weren't considered a slut with all your loose talk, well, you were seen, at the very least, as a lousy housewife and mother. Attacks on gossip in the sixteenth and seventeenth centuries often focused on the fact that it took women away from the housework and the family. "Gossip's association with a community of women outside the domestic sphere challenged male ideals of submissive domestic behaviour and the idea that the housewife's main responsibility was to her immediate family," writes Aldershot.

Duh. What do you think girls' weekends are all about, silly?

The Secret Language Is Born

So what's a girl to do? Stop talking? I don't think so. Sure, maybe once upon a time the only women permitted to speak in public were queens and prophets. And so what if Catholic and Protestant marriage manuals used to define the ideal wife as "obedient, silent, and pious," according to Merry E. Weisner's *Women and Gender in Early Modern Europe*? Somehow, ordinary women found plenty of places to talk among themselves. They just learned to talk when the men weren't around. "Women spent a great deal of time together, and during that time they talked," writes Weisner.

"Around the well, at the mill, in a spinning circle, and at the bed of a newly delivered mother, women discussed subjects from fertility to royalty," write Natalie Zemon Davis and Arlette Farge in *A History of Women in the West: Renaissance and Enlightenment Paradoxes*. "Here were exchanged the '*secrètes* of women.'" In other words, despite centuries of male attempts to shut us up, women kept right on yammering. In fact, attempts to keep us quiet only strengthened communication among women by bolstering female bonding and the Secret Language of Girls.

Despite the important role it played in women's lives, however, women's talk was still not taken seriously. The way women talked was dismissed as an inferior form of conversation, lacking the significance of men's words. Consider this quotation from Davis and Farge on working-class women in Glasgow: "When women discuss 'the treatment you get from the doctor these days,' 'waiting for operations,' 'damp in the back bedroom,' and 'the price of a loaf,' they are more likely to be perceived as immersed in idle gossip rather than political comment. The trade union member who complains of 'treatment from supervisors,' 'fumes in the paint shop,' 'cold on the shop floor,' and 'cuts in wages' is viewed rather differently."

Which just makes you mad.

But, again, if the boys didn't take us seriously, we did what we'd been doing for centuries: found other women to talk to who understood, shared our perspective, and took our so-called superficial concerns seriously.

The Private Goes Public

Though women's talk of children, domestic affairs, and relationships was seen as frivolous, sexually scandalous, or igno-
rant, women understood its value. (We know that even the
most silly night out with the girls is of utmost importance in
our lives). At the same time, women knew by now that they
weren't going to get their perspective out into the world
through traditionally male outlets; that, as usual, talking to
each other was often more productive than trying to convince men they had something important to say.

Women in revolutionary France at the end of the eighteenth century were not permitted full membership in revolutionary organizations. So, in at least thirty cities, according
to Dominique Godineau in *A History of Women in the West:
Emerging Feminism from Revolution to World War*, they formed
their own clubs. The members of these clubs met regularly to
discuss the laws and newspapers, to debate local and national
political issues, and to engage in philanthropic activities.
And they did it their way. "Women gathered to gossip and
exchange news (and sometimes blows)," writes Godineau.

"During the Revolution these encounters took on a political colouration: the laundresses who met in taverns when
their day's work was done together deciphered the speeches
of revolutionary orators. Neighbours who had set their chairs
on their doorsteps to savour a sweet summer's night came to
blows when one championed the cause of the Girondins, the

other of the Montagnards. Women were apt to share their political views with women neighbours rather than with their husbands; sometimes neighbours went arm in arm, chatting gaily or 'fiercely,' to the legislative galleries."

Beyond politics, women found other ways to take their Secret Language public. According to art historian Anne Higonnet, the amateur art of women at the end of the late nineteenth and early twentieth centuries was rife with domestic images of family, home, and other women. Domestic chores created forums for women to bond, communicate, and even organize.

Quilting bees are probably one of the most famous examples of this. Joan Mulholland talks about the role of the quilting bee in a 1996 *Journal of American Culture* article. From the earliest white settlement in America, quilting bees existed as a communal event. Because bed quilts were so large, a good deal of sewing was required to complete them. So women set up sewing circles at their homes, calling friends and neighbours to join. "To make the quilting time pass, the women talked. They related their experiences, shared problems, offered advice, and probably disputed, negotiated, and argued."

If hubby wanted to stay warm in winter, this was one instance where he had to accept the gathering of women. The best he could hope for was that the quilt would provide enough of a focus for the group to avoid engaging in "dangerous gossip."

No such luck. "The talking done at the bee solidified the group's identity, and the relationship of its members, as well as providing a platform on which women could practice a form of public speech," writes Mulholland. It is now a famous part of women's history that Susan B. Anthony, one of the leaders of the American women's rights movement, made her first speech at a quilting bee.

The "F" Word Becomes Part of the Secret Language

Modern feminism really brought the Secret Language out of the closet, or the kitchen, as it were. You might say the consciousness-raising groups of the seventies served as the quilting bees of our time.

During this era, feminism also expanded the vocabulary of the Secret Language, giving it new words, symbols, and codes. Terms like "the Sisterhood" finally defined what women had been doing for years: bonding over common ground and taking the private and personal and making it public and political.

Throughout Western Europe and North America, the symbol ♀ for female became an icon for women's solidarity and power. A clenched fist within the symbol's circle came to signify female power. In Europe, demonstrating feminists substituted a hand-formed vulva for the clenched fist as another way of indicating women's separateness from male politics and emphasizing their own power.

The Secret Language was marching out into the public sphere and being shouted out loud. "Over the years a phraseology laden with political overtones emerged to jibe with feminist analyses of women's conditions," writes Yasmine Ergas in her book *A History of Women in the West*. "'Sisterhood' served to indicate the strength (and quasi-genetic roots) of feminist solidarity. Other key terms, such as 'patriarchy,' stood for the pervasiveness of male domination and female oppression that justified women's rebellion. This language solidified the movements' bonds."

Of course, women-only spaces existed from the first time the boys left the cave to go off and kill some wild boar, but modern feminism saw the first conscious effort to create women-only spaces that formally acknowledged that, well, we have a different way of getting together from the lads.

The Secret Language of Girls was finally finding an official place out in the world. However, the early feminists wanted little to do with the private, domestic worlds where the Secret Language first took hold. Seventies' feminism was all about getting women out of the kitchen and into the working world. It was about freedom from the perceived chains of femininity. If women couldn't be taken seriously as homemakers and mothers, well, godammit, we'd just condemn those choices for women. Eventually, we came to realize that this wasn't so practical. Without homemakers and mothers, well, we'd not only put a damper on the continuity of the human race, we'd also have to live with *his* notion of "clean enough."

But it took feminism and a rejection of these expected and often trivialized roles to arrive at where we are today: a place where we can make the choice. And where we can appreciate that the pleasure and camaraderie derived from engaging in traditionally female activities is not trivial or silly but powerful and rejuvenating.

It's a place where I can pick up a copy of *Bust*—a feminist magazine—and find an article titled "A Broom of One's Own" about one woman's liberating journey from Betty Friedan to Betty Crocker. The article's author, Jean Railla, who says she was raised "a good feminist," talks about how she was taught that housework was drudgery—work done by women who didn't know better. "Smart, enlightened women became artists, writers, thinkers; they became important. They didn't have time for silly things like cooking, sewing, knitting or cleaning. . . . The logic of the day was: work/career is good; home/domesticity is bad."

Given the high female viewership for all those cooking and home decorating shows on television today, it would seem we're getting over that kinda thinking. I'm not saying we should all head back into the kitchen, unless of course it's to gather around the table with your best girlfriends, a bottle of wine, and some salty snacks. While I adore many things traditionally considered female (well, ironing and washing floors I could live without), I don't want to be limited to these choices. But I'm glad that we've finally realized that domestic things are not necessarily bad or female and that chick things are being celebrated rather than trivialized.

And after centuries of being excluded from the boys' club, a lot of us are realizing we simply have more fun with the girls. While men may dismiss our gatherings, we don't care any more because we know they secretly wish they could be a fly on the wall.

I love that when I see my girlfriends, we can, in one breath, gush over one another's outfits, and in the next, share deep personal and emotional insights about our relationships, our place in the world, what so-and-so is doing, and what we'll make for dinner together. And we will understand each other profoundly.

This Secret Language gives me a life. In their book, *Feminism ManifestA: Young Women, Feminism, and the Future*, authors Jennifer Baumgardner and Amy Richards (both former editors of Ms. magazine) describe the ideal dinner party, where Mary Magdalene would discuss sex workers' rights, Lilith would give first wives' advice to Eve—who would finally recognize that she'd been framed.

"The concept for this chapter ["The Dinner Party"] came out of a fierce faith that this honest communicating among women is a revolutionary act, and the best preface to activism," write the authors. "Of course, not all dinner parties are intentionally subversive. Women also use these gatherings as an excuse to sit down and talk about some interesting stranger they admire, or to develop ideas by having intellectual trysts with other women. . . . This need to get together for girl talk begins over soggy Tater Tots in the grade-school cafeteria, continues through endless confabs on the phone or on sports teams during high school and is grabbed throughout adulthood in book clubs or beauty parlors, while lifting weights at the gym or running through Target or at work."

Yes, "girl talk," despite being criticized, demeaned, dismissed, and dragged through the mud for centuries, bonds us more than ever. Even words once used against us have been recast in the dictionary of the Secret Language, giving them new and powerful meanings that no longer allow them to be used to hurt us. Suffragist, bra burner, and women's libber have all lost their impact as put-downs, Baumgardner and Richards tell us. "Girl, bitch, slut, and cunt—all of which are titles of records and books by feminists of our generation—are no longer scary words we have to keep in the closet, in fear that they become weapons to be deployed against us."

Despite centuries of trying to undermine and eradicate female communication, the Secret Language of Girls is alive and well and stronger than ever. In a recent *New York Times* article about women's groups and girl talk, author Rachel Lehmann-Haupt points out that "part career networking and romance therapy, part retro kaffeeklatsch, a new genre of women's groups has been emerging—one that emphasizes the role of gossip and 'girl talk' as much as weightier subjects in the life of the nineties' woman."

Now we have TV programs like *The View* and *Sex and the City* and Web-based communities like iVillage and Chickclick all trumpeting what I call the Secret Language of Girls.

It's a language that most of us begin to learn early in life.

What Little Girls Are Made Of

Father Knows Best, my ass. That may have been the case in TV land, but we all know that in reality, when you really want the answers, you go to Mom. Especially if you're a little girl. Sure, Dad's around, maybe. But he doesn't get blamed for screwing up our lives until we start dating men who are like our fathers. Mom, on the other hand is under scrutiny from day one.

In a recent study by smartgirl.com, 79 per cent of girls aged eight to twelve say that Mom is their top source of advice, while only 41 per cent seek out their father's counsel. Dr. Ellen Silber, a director of the Marymount Institute for the Education of Women and Girls in Tarrytown, New York, says that a girl's relationship with her mother is the most important one that shapes who she is.

Whew, no pressure there.

There was a time when Mom's teachings were the only education a young woman got. In *A Daughter to Educate*, Martine Sonnet indicates that home was the only school for girls of the sixteenth century. "Most learned at home watching their mothers go about her daily chores," she writes. Lessons included cooking, child care, washing, mending, sewing, and weaving. Mending may not be the pinnacle of womanhood it once was, and certainly educational opportunities for women have advanced somewhat since then. But whatever the era and whatever the advice, Mom is our first example of what's in store for us as women, of how to "do" girl. She is our blueprint. Our first teacher of the Secret Language of Girls.

Because women are made of the same genetic code, the mother/daughter connection is much stronger, says thirty-one-year old Meredith, who was raised by a single mom and knows only too well how intense the mother/daughter bond can be. "When her daughter is going through puberty, for example, a mother feels she's been through that and knows what her daughter is feeling," says Meredith. "She wants to be there to hold her hand and walk her through it."

However, sometimes Mom fails to recognize that the two of you are different people, and the daughter's struggle to assert this distinction can get ugly. When it's just you and Mom, it can get even uglier. "The problem with single mothers is that the relationship with her child, particularly a girl, can be quite intense," according to Meredith. "Sometimes that relationship becomes more primary to the mother than the child.

Often, my mother can't see the line between where she ends and I begin. She read my diary when I was a child, and her violation of my privacy remains an ongoing problem."

Sometimes my own mother knows me better than I know myself. "You could never live in the country again," she says of my on-again/off-again fantasy of moving back to the sticks, where I grew up. "You'd be bored," she states matter-of-factly. Part of me resents her assumed authority on the subject of me. But at the same time I know she's right. And there's comfort in knowing that when I lose my way, she'll know what's best for me.

So while we fight to separate ourselves from our mothers, we crave our mother's approval and understanding. It's a confusing dynamic, but once we learn it, it's a pattern that we repeat over and over again in our relationships with other women.

Our gender and experience bond us while our struggle to be separate pits us against each other. The conflict between the two constantly messes us up.

Mommie Dearest?

My mom was forty when she had me. I remember being envious of other girls whose younger mothers seemed more like friends than moms. But my mom didn't come from an era where her mother was her friend. Her mother taught her what she needed to know about how to be a good mother and wife. Mom was a good learner as she did a kick-ass job—trust me, living on a farm with eight kids, it was a full-time gig.

The shift from mother as teacher/authoritarian to friend/confidante is a relatively new development in the mother/daughter world. In *Conversations with Mothers and Daughters*, Celia Dodd explains how previous generations' love for their mothers was often tinged with fear and respect. Friendship was not part of the equation. This shift was first encouraged in magazines like the *Ladies' Home Journal*, which published the following in 1884 (its first year of publication): "It is the companionable mothers who are the only ones to keep their girls' confidences." This was no doubt tough for women who were not friends with their own mothers. Without a satisfactory role model, says Dodd, many mothers struggled to achieve the kind of companionable relationship with their daughters that was suddenly expected. During the late nineteenth and early twentieth century, articles, editorials and advice columns implied that serious problems existed in the area of mother/daughter relationships.

Shifting times and more opportunities for women outside the home meant that daughters began to have attitudes and experiences that were different from their mothers'. As a result, what Mom passes along can sometimes seem a little out of step. "Marry a rich man" and "Your boobs will sag when you get old, so enjoy them now," were two nuggets of advice twenty-nine-year-old Tammy, a freelance writer, got from her mom. This, Tammy was told, was everything she needed to know about being a woman.

With educational opportunities increasing, many young women decided they wanted their intellects to shine more than their kitchen floors and went off to university or college, furthering the gap between mother and daughter. "When I was young and still in the mother-worship stage, I wanted to be like her," says thirty-seven-year-old Karen, who has a bachelor's degree in education and was the first female on her mother's side of the family to attend university. "Then, during the teen years, I thought she was a fool for wasting her life as a housewife, a role that I equated with drudgery. My mother was always good at communicating feelings—like why she was mad, hurt, annoyed or bothered by something," Karen continues. "She wasn't, however, very good at articulating ideas or philosophies, and I sometimes got the sense that she tuned out when I discussed things like that. It's a weird feeling when you realize you've intellectually outgrown your mother. Now when we talk, I often feel like I'm pontificating rather than sharing ideas."

A Model Mom

Yet despite the often-troubled relationships so many of us have with our mothers, I was struck by how many women described their mother as their strongest female role model growing up.

My mother is one of the strongest, most resilient women I know. The lessons I have learned from her about being a woman are many—some have helped more than others. She was a devoted parent who worked hard, was always there for us, never complained, and only occasionally lost it when we tried her patience. I can still see her chasing us with a hairbrush and quickly laughing at her own outrage. Many of her qualities I see in myself.

Ruschelle, a twenty-year-old student, describes her mother as a strong and independent woman, and Ruschelle is happy to be following her lead. "She had four kids and worked as a social worker at the same time, which is why I'm studying to be a social worker," she tells me. "When I was growing up in Boston, my mother would take in people who had nowhere else to go—I really admired that."

Celeste, a twenty-five-year-old youth centre co-ordinator, also cites her mother as her biggest influence and inspiration. "She came to Canada from Trinidad without much of anything and was able to make herself a success. As a single woman, she was able to purchase her own house. When she married my dad and he moved into the house, he asked, 'So who do we pay rent to?' and she answered, 'Me.'" This year, Celeste bought her own condo. "My mom's proud of me," she says, beaming.

Mom passes along, through examples and words, how we should look and act, what we should wear, how we should relate to men, and how to relate to women. Mom's messages can be confusing. On one hand, she shows us the importance of relying on other women; on the other hand, she shows us that as women, we are defined by our ability to attract men and that we must compete with other women for a good man. She tells us we can be or do anything we want. When society tells us we can't, we feel a little betrayed by her.

Yet we are protective of our mothers. At any cost. "My older sister told me never to do anything that could hurt our mother," Donna, a public relations executive in her early forties, tells me. "So I lied through my teeth. All the time." Subsequently, we are protective of other women in our lives, even if it means softening the truth once in a while.

Although I learned of the strength of women from my mom, I also learned never to complain and to take care of everybody else before myself; that men and boys get seconds first; that girls do housework while boys work outside; and that women say things like "I shouldn't" before putting anything into their mouths.

Admittedly, Mom doesn't always feel like the best plan to be working from. Yet the examples we see and the lessons we learn from our mothers truly do shape who we become. And even if we fight against our mother's ideas of femininity and run screaming in the other direction to do everything not to be like her, inevitably one day, as adults, we do or say something and think, Oh my God, I sound just like my mother!

The intimacy we share with our mothers is one we take out into the world and re-create with girlfriends, lovers, partners, and eventually, if we so choose, our children. It's a complex intimacy but one that we take comfort in. The contradictions we endure in our relationship with our mother establish a solid base for the lifelong contradictions that most women live with daily.

Mom is our friend. She makes us feel safe. She is our ally in a world still dominated by men. She is our defender. We are proud of her. But she can also embarrass us. She is our (s)mother. Or she isn't there for us enough. Then we hate our mother. She is crazy. She makes us crazy. She lives her life through us. We compete with our mother for our father's love.

On top of all this, we need Mom simply to be a mom: to be there for us, to be our comfort and solace, to catch us when we fall and to fulfill our every need.

Oh, and could she be cool too, please?

No wonder women learn to be such great multi-taskers.

Circle of Friends

Many women I spoke with have fond memories of their mothers and her sisters and/or girlfriends sitting around kitchen tables kvetching, laughing, gossiping, and consoling one another. Early on we learn how important it is to have a network of women in our lives.

Celeste, like a lot of women who come from West Indian families, calls her mom's friends "Auntie." In other words, Mom's friends are part of the family. It's a long-standing tradition. "The mid-nineteenth-century girl spent most of her time in the company of women. Her world was composed of and defined by her mother, her mother's friends and relatives, her sisters and her own girlfriends," writes Nancy M. Theriot in *Mothers and Daughters in Nineteenth-Century America: The Biosocial Construction of Femininity*.

It was not always a choice. Jennifer-Lynn, a twenty-five-year-old freelance writer who grew up on a farm as an only child, says that women in her family often gathered around quilting bees or to share the cooking duties. "That's when the women of the family got together to complain, talk, and generally hang out," she says. "It was more of a forced-together type of bonding than something they chose to do. Similar to men at war, I guess." She also got a clear message that this female company should never get in the way of your boyfriend or husband. Unless the bastard takes off with another woman.

Jenny, an editor in her late twenties, remembers the strength her mother drew from her close female friends when Jenny's father left for another woman. "They rallied around her in a big way. I remember a lot of pep talks, crying on shoulders, that sort of thing." Watching this bond in action as little girls, we learn why women need and enjoy the company of women, not just to get us through times of crisis, but also to share our most intimate secrets.

When Sarah, a thirty-eight-year-old senior producer at an Internet design company, was growing up in England, she knew that when her mother had her female friends over for "coffee," this was code for private talk time. "They'd go in the kitchen and shut the door, and we knew that it was a private conversation." Kitchens have always been one of the most popular gathering places for women. I loved sitting around the kitchen table with my mother, sisters and aunts waiting for a meal to cook or after the dishes were done. Even now, one of my most favourite things to do with my girlfriends is to hang out in the kitchen and cook dinner together while polishing off a bottle of wine. As far as I'm concerned, food and booze are essential fuel for female friendships.

Donna, who comes from an Italian family, agrees. "Women and food were a huge part of my life. They still are," she says. "I remember the women in my family as a veritable coven of witches—assorted aunts, cousins, friends of the family, hovering over huge pots in the kitchen—making food like homemade cannelloni and ravioli."

Women come up with any excuse to kick back and enjoy a little down time together. When Celeste's mother first came to Canada, she was a working mom who needed her ritual 3 A.M. Scrabble fests with her new Canadian girlfriends to get comfy. The bottle of wine they shared helped. Celeste also remembers Tupperware and lingerie parties among the many excuses they had to get together.

Like rewarding yourselves at the end of a good day's work. "I remember my mom and her best friend sitting around in the afternoon—after the house was cleaned and chores were done—sipping sherry, watching *The Edge of Night*, gossiping, and sharing recipes at the commercial breaks," recalls Lisa, a thirty-five-year-old performance artist and graphic designer.

SHEROES:
GALS WHO INSPIRED US GROWING UP

Mary Tyler Moore and *That Girl*—Marlo Thomas. I loved that they had their own apartments, good friends, and interesting jobs. They were successful on their own. What was that song on the *MTM* show? "You're Gonna Make It After All." – Barb, 39

I really respected Björk. I remember reading about her telling her son anarchist bedtime stories, which I thought was really cool. – Aimee, 24

I looooved Riff Randall in the movie *Rock 'n' Roll High School*. She was smart and sassy, not preppy, and all the boys still wanted her. She had rock 'n' roll goals and knew how to get what she wanted. – Fateema, 22

Nadia Comaneci. I wanted to be a gymnast so badly that I held her in high regard even though she was younger than me. – Karen, 37

I had an aunt in Germany who ran her own heating oil business. She always wore red Coco Chanel-type suits with red kid gloves, red shoes, and red lipstick. She loved to drink wine and eat smoked eel and paint my toenails red. – Lisa, 35

Wonder Woman. She was an Amazon princess and she had an invisible plane! – Jenny, 25

Jaclyn Smith as a Charlie's Angel; she was smart, beautiful and she kicked ass. – Jackie, 33

I wanted to be a rock star, so when I was a kid most of my role models were male. When I discovered Tori Amos and Sarah McLachlan, I really started admiring women. – Andie, 20

My mother. She raised three children alone, and we all turned out relatively normal. She was very strong, physically and emotionally. She could change the oil in the car, perfectly iron a dress shirt, and make home-cooked dinners. – Kimberly, 29

Oprah. I relate to a lot of the issues she's worked through: low self-esteem, body image, and depression. Plus she's a successful woman of colour. – Sapna, 27

Nancy Drew. She was together, smart, and had lots of freedom to pursue what she wanted. She had all kinds of fabulous adventures while making the world right for people. – Lydia, 34

Anne of Green Gables. She was a tough, smart, and imaginative person who was not afraid to speak her mind. – Amy, 25

My grandmother. She is intelligent, witty, and prepared to do anything for her family. I admire her strength and the fact that she has always gone against stereotypes.

She went to NYU in the 1930s and worked even after she had children. – Erica, 19

Miss Piggy from *The Muppets*. She was beautiful, outspoken and glamorous, and she always got what she wanted. – Erin, 25

Laura Ingalls from *Little House on the Prairie*. I loved her defiance, her toughness in the face of adversity, and how loving she was. She defended and helped her sisters and hated sewing and all the girl traps of the time. I was inspired by the fact that she was a woman who wrote and published books. – Roxanne, 22

Madonna. She does whatever the hell she wants and doesn't give a damn what people think of her. She freely expresses her sexuality. She is an incredible businesswoman. When she wanted to have a baby, she did it without having to get married. – Krista, 19

Courtney Love. I admire her fierceness, her balls, and her strength. She never backs down from anything, she inspires me to face life—head-on, to go down fighting. – Tiffany, 18

Hatshepsut. She was the only female pharaoh that we know about. She dared to assume power in a misogynist world. – Maribelle, 33

Pippi Longstocking. She was independent and didn't care what people thought. – Angel, 30

Getting together with the girls was also a time for Mom to bitch about Dad with her friends. Donna remembers her mom and aunts laughing together and talking about their husbands. "It was like a secretive, close intimate bonding," she says.

It was also a chance for our mothers to let their hair down and be themselves for a few hours, something many women of our mothers' generation didn't always get a chance to enjoy. "I learned that they had one type of relationship when men weren't around and a quieter, more submissive role when men were," adds Donna.

Amy, a thirty-one-year-old stay-at-home mom, points out that in the company of other women, we are most often the women we most want to be: "With women it's safe to be funny and clever and real."

Sugar and Spice

While Mom was our first teacher, she eventually let us out of her clutches and sent us off to school, where many more lessons in the Secret Language of Girls were learned.

I went to a small country Catholic school: two classrooms, six grades. Boys played on one side of the yard, girls on the other. Recesses for us girls involved skipping and playing baseball on the crummy, swampy diamond without a catcher's back fence while the boys played on the good diamond complete with fence and real bases. I was called a hussy one day for playing on the boys' side of the yard. I learned my lesson: girls and boys don't mix. We used to whine about it once in a while, but mostly I enjoyed hanging with the girls. We played ball our way and didn't have stupid boys to deal with.

Barrie Thorne, a sociology professor at Berkeley and author of *Gender Play: Girls and Boys in School*, was surprised by how quickly kids separate by sex on the playground, even when there aren't adults around to call them hussies if they play with the boys. "Boys seemed to control the large fixed spaces designated for team sports: baseball diamonds, grassy fields used for football or soccer," she says. "The spaces girls predominated—bars and jungle gyms and painted cement areas for playing foursquare, jump rope and hopscotch— were closer to the building and much smaller, taking up per- haps a tenth of the territory that boys controlled."

They may take up less space, but what was clear to Thorne was that girls make sure the space they do take up belongs only to them. Thorne relates the story of a Grade 1 boy named Evan who would often sit and watch the girls skip- ping. One time when the girls were deciding who would turn the rope (the yucky job), Evan decided this would be his in. "I'll swing it," he offered. But a girl named Julie quickly shut him out. "No way—you don't know how to do it. You gotta be a girl," she said.

Turns out girls don't always want to be included with the boys on the playground. They relish the company of other girls, just because, well, they're girls. Researchers believe that most children's awareness that one is a girl or a boy consolidates around age two. That awareness, some suggest, may lead girls to want to be with girls and boys with boys. "Being with those of 'one's own kind' and avoiding those of 'the other kind' confirms 'girlness' or 'boyness' and fills a need for self discovery," according to Thorne.

Seven-year-old Sarah puts it simply for me. "I like having girlfriends better because I'm a girl, so it's like we're the same." It also makes being bossy easier. Several studies have shown that girls stick together when they are little in part because they have found that, at as young as age three, they can influence other girls but have difficulty influencing boys, whereas boys tend to be successful in influencing both boys and girls. "This might lead girls to avoid boys and turn their attention to girls," Thorne suggests. "In short, girls, at least initially, may separate from boys in order to avoid being dominated."

Or to avoid having to be "it" all the time. "When I play tag with the boys at recess, they run faster," Sarah tells me, "so I'm always 'it.'"

You Play like a Girl!

Once you have the girls and boys in their own worlds, it's fascinating to see what goes on; it's like one big girls' night.

Girls affirm solidarity and commonality, says Vivian Gussin Paley, a former kindergarten teacher and author of

Boys and Girls: Superheroes in the Doll Corner. On school playgrounds, "girls are less likely than boys to play team sports," writes Paley. "They more often engage in small-scale, turn-taking and cooperative kinds of play. By fifth and sixth grade, many of them spend recess standing around and talking. When they jump rope or play on the bars, girls take turns performing and watching others perform in stylized movements that may involve considerable skill."

Thorne also observed these differences on the playground. She watched girls work out group choreographies, counting and jumping rope in unison. Grade 5 and 6 girls practiced cheerleading routines or dance steps.

In a 1996 interview in *Wired* magazine, Doug Glen, the president of Mattel, talked about experimenting with superhero toys for girls. In their research, the company asked kids to tell them a story of what the superhero would do once he or she faced his or her archenemy. Glen said the boys would explain in gory detail how they'd draw and quarter the archenemy and do all sorts of horrendous things to finish him off. The girls wanted to rehabilitate him. And while transformation is a big thing for all kids, boys usually want to transform from something less powerful to something more powerful (think superhero) and girls want to become glamorous and magical (think Ugly Duckling and Cinderella).

Anthropologist Helen Fisher believes some of these differences again go back to our ancestors. "Boys tend to form hierarchies and then jockey for position," she tells me. "They live in a world of win/lose." Girls, on the other hand, tend to live more in a world of win/win, Fisher says. "They form cliques and are constantly trying to be liked. They are very busy trying to build a web of connections and then use these support systems."

And while boys like to stick to the rules, girls are more likely to bend the rules when someone's emotions are at stake. Even at this stage, we've already learned how to keep everyone happy. (Thanks, Mom.) This becomes even more evident in traditionally boy-dominated areas of play, like sport. According to the Canadian Association for the Advancement of Women in Sports, 61 per cent of boys aged five to fourteen are active in sports compared with only 41 per cent of girls.

Sydney Millar, the national co-ordinator for CAAWS's On the Move program, which is designed to get girls more physically active, says that while there are certainly girls who are as athletic and competitive as boys, most girls don't enjoy the competitive nature of sports. "Girls enjoy sports that are more co-operative and social." Boys, on the other hand, socialize through competitive sports. Boys don't go over to each other's homes to paint each other's nails; they go over and play basketball. Girls also quickly realize that being a "jock" won't make you popular or sexy with boys, says Millar, who herself was one of only about ten girls in her school of 200 to 250 who she says "came out" as "jocks."

You see the differences in how boys and girls play with video games as well, another arena dominated by boys. Most computer game technology is based on response games, blowing stuff up and getting to the next level, says Sheri Graner Ray, president of Sirenia Software, a company dedicated to producing "technically sophisticated, fun games for girls."

"Studies have shown boys like visual stimulus that presents conflict and brings it to a head, and they like the conflict resolution to involve sprayed guts, or something fast with lots of movement and colour, like car chases, explosions, and gore," she explains. "Girls will choose negotiation, compromise, diplomacy and manipulation that lead to an emotional resolution. They want to know why they're shooting at that guy and what good it does to blow him out of the sky." Girls don't like these games not because they are "gory" or "yucky," she adds, but because they get bored beating on the same character over and over again for no reason that they can see.

Obviously these are all generalizations. There are plenty of examples of girls who want to draw and quarter their dolls and boys who like to skip rope, like poor Evan. But I am constantly amazed at how this pattern generally holds up. Many mothers who grew up feminists talk about how they desperately tried to expose their sons and daughters to male and female forms of play. But as one mother said to me, "I don't get my boys. They're destructive—all they want to do is seek and destroy—and they're all about active energy. They don't want to sit quietly and just chat or draw. It's frustrating, whereas my girlfriend's little girls will sit and draw for hours and hours."

Vivian, a former kindergarten teacher whom I spoke to, says she saw it over and over again—the girls go to house things and the boys go to the sandbox. As for how much of this behaviour is biological, hormonal or socialized, the jury it still out. There's no denying that we still tend to dote on little girls and tell them they're pretty while we play rougher with little boys. And we still make plenty of assumptions based on gender.

Susan Herring, the Berkeley professor I mentioned last chapter who studied female communication online, told me about a study in which adult students were asked to identify the reactions of a nine-month-old baby to a jack-in-the-box. Half the students were told the baby was a girl, and half were told a boy. The students who thought the baby was a girl said she looked afraid when she saw the jack-in-the-box. The students who thought the baby was a boy thought he looked angry. We don't expect little girls to get angry. It's not lady-like, of course. Girls are rewarded for keeping their anger to themselves and for being nice. So a lot of us work really hard at niceness.

Donna still remembers the reaction she got for being assertive as a young girl. "I was always a leader and spoke my mind," she says. "My kindergarten teacher wrote that I was 'bossy' on my report card. Other girls were quiet and passive—and frustrated! However, they received adult approval."

Not So Nice

Girls may learn the importance of being nice, but that doesn't mean they're all sugar and spice. There is plenty of conflict and tension underneath all that co-operation and group harmony. Girls can be just as aggressive as young boys. They just learn to be sneakier about it. Thorne talks about girls playing foursquare on the playground competing in a co-operative way, using language of "being friends" and "being nice" while aggressively getting others out so their friends could play.

A male friend of mine remembers this type of behaviour. When he was a kid, he liked to skip with the girls. Oddly enough, he says, it wasn't the boys who had a problem with it. "I saw more flak coming from the girls who would ostracize the other girls who let me play." Girls even bully less directly than boys, according to researchers. While boys will call each other names and are more likely to be physically rough, girls will be mean by excluding other girls.

Amy Sheldon is a professor in speech communication at the University of Minnesota who videotaped young children at play in a local daycare. She says girls use what she describes as a "double-voice style." In interacting with one another, girls tried to avoid the appearance of hierarchy and overt conflict while plenty of conflict, self-assertion, and even aggression went on beneath the surface. In one case, Sheldon taped groups of three-year-old boys and girls fighting over a plastic pickle. The dispute in the group of boys got physical

LET'S PLAY DOLL

I loved hopscotch. I played a mean game of house as a child, and I looooved my Barbies. I begged for the Barbie Camper and Dune Buggy and had an Easy Bake Oven. Did that make me a manipulated little girl destined to a life of domesticity? Or an adventurer who loved to go camping and had a sweet tooth that I could satisfy by whipping up a cake under the glowing bulb of my Easy Bake?

Girls get a lot of flak for playing with "girl stuff," especially Barbie. So many women I know were forbidden to play with Barbie or embarrassed to admit that they did. I find this sad. After all, I managed to grow up with Barbie and not desire blond hair and a thirteen-inch waist. Personally, I think those who think Barbie is a bad role model have it all wrong. We learned so much from Barbie.

"She is an icon of improvisation," write Justine Cassell and Henry Jenkins in *From Barbie to Mortal Kombat*. "Barbie perpetually performs so as to become whatever the situation demands—a venturesome camper, a capable babysitter, a fashionable shopper . . . her dreams, her passions, her abiding attachments remain a mystery."

As Jennifer Baumgardner and Amy Richards point out in their book *ManifestA*, "We didn't want to be our dolls; we just wanted to cut their hair, make them go out on dates, and swim in the Barbie pool with Skipper."

And make her have sex, of course. Barbie was the first sexually liberated woman I knew. She did it whenever she wanted to, however she wanted to, and wherever she wanted to, and Ken just had to go along with it. Though, in my case, I didn't have a Ken doll, so Barbie encouraged my first experimentation with lesbianism.

Despite her supposed failings, Barbie was also one of the first gals to get little girls excited about computers. Barbie Designer was one of the first successful girl computer games selling half a million units from October 1996 to March 1997.

"I don't think a program that designs dresses will make girls want to be engineers," admits Sheri Graner Ray, president of Sirenia Software. "But it will be one tool in their belt. They'll like computers and see them as friendly."

It might be time to rethink Barbie's "bad role model" image. After all, as Baumgardner and Richards point out, "Besides the lifestyle choices imposed on Barbie from her diverse, possibly perverse, owners, the forty-one-year-old doll has had some seventy-four careers, some of which broke occupational barriers that flesh-and-blood women are still just scratching at."

almost immediately. They grabbed the pickle, got angry, pushed each other around, and raised their voices. But the conflict was resolved quickly and they went back to playing with no apparent hurt feelings.

The girls also argued, but less overtly, and the dispute went on much longer. At one point, one of the girls suggested they divide the pickle in three parts so that everyone could have some. It was all a pretext because in the process the little girl nabbed the pickle. To top it off, the pickle was actually made of plastic, so it couldn't be divided. It was an interesting strategy because while it promoted the idea of social harmony and sharing, it was ultimately more manipulative. Clever, huh?

Thick as Thieves

The patterns of adult female friendships can already be seen on the playground. Vivian, the former kindergarten teacher I spoke with, tells me that in the classroom girls establish a best friend within the first month of school and are as "thick as thieves together," whereas boys continue to play beside each other rather than together.

Girls even talk about friendships differently from boys, says *Gender Play* author Barrie Thorne. According to her observations, boys tend to talk about "buddies," "teams," and "being tough" while girls more often talk about "best friends" and "being nice."

And boys tend to hang out in groups or packs early on, while girls typically form pairs of "best friends." That's not to say that these arrangements don't shift. If you've ever wondered how adult women's friendships became so complicated, again, just look to the schoolyard. It is an ever-changing world of shifting alliances, cliques, and exclusionary practices.

"Girls often participate in two or more pairs of 'best friends' at one time, resulting in complex social networks," says Thorne. "Girls often talk about who is 'best friends with,' 'likes,' or is 'being mean to' whom." Relationships between friends sometimes break off, and girls hedge bets by structuring networks of potential friends. And much of the activity of making and breaking friends and forming new alliances is done through third parties. Just like big girls.

"The worst thing is when they're really mean to me and call me names and say they don't want to hang around with me any more," seven-and-a-half-year-old (she was very adamant about the half!) Jennifer tells me.

"Sometimes you get in a bit of a fight and you don't hang out with them any more—and it's like they've all had a meeting and decided let's not be nice to Jen."

"I had this one friend who was cruel and manipulative. But I adored her," recalls Donna. "She pitted all her friends against each other, but she always had friends. She was the first to have everything—colour TV, cable, go-go boots, fad toys, board games—and the first to go on wild exotic trips with her parents. Her father had a big burgundy Le Sabre sedan; my dad had a brown Rambler. It was humiliating try-ing to keep up with her. My sweetest revenge was that she was dumb as a doorknob at school and I got straight A's."

Jennifer, thirty-one, tells me that when she was little, she and her best friend even drew up a contract that they taped to the insides of their desks stating that they always had to be each other's partner at school or for anything else. "We even had a protocol about illness, in which we had another girl who we picked out as an acceptable substitute if one of us was sick," she remembers.

Seven-year-old Jennifer explains the importance of girl-friends: "I need my friends to talk to, and I need my girlfriends when I'm sad or lonely. Sometimes when I have a fight with a friend, another friend will help us get back together." Not only do little girls need the emotional closeness of other girls already at this age, but they are also often more physically close than boys. In gestures of intimacy that one rarely sees among boys, girls stroke or comb their friends' hair, says Thorne.

Or bathe together. "My best friend and I used to have baths together and create games with the sponges," says thirty-eight-year-old Sarah. "It was a very intimate bonding experience, and we entered our own little secret world. We were both devastated when her mother decided we were too old to bathe together."

And sometimes that intimacy does lend itself nicely to some innocent experimentation. "I remember practicing kissing with my two friends," says twenty-nine-year-old

Adele. "It would start with each of us kissing our own dolls. Then we would practice our holding techniques on our pillows, and when we realized this just wasn't going to give us the practical experience we needed, we started kissing each other. When we started doing the 'icky tongue thing,' we came to the conclusion that we might be getting ahead of ourselves."

This type of exploration doesn't always go over so well, which can be a little confusing at times. "When I was in Grade 2, my friend and I used to play these make-out games and do 'grown-up things,'" twenty-year-old Jessika recalls. "It was totally normal and cool for me to be doing this with this girl. Until I played 'house' with another girl, and when I went to kiss her she said, 'My mom doesn't want me to do those things.' I didn't understand why but I just left it at that."

Even at this age, says Thorne, little girls notice and comment on one anothers' physical appearance (such as haircuts and clothes) and borrow and wear sweaters or sweatshirts. Best friends monitor one anothers' emotions. They share secrets and become mutually vulnerable by telling each other things about themselves they would never tell anyone else. A Canadian Teachers Federation study found that while girls are concerned about succeeding in school and their futures, they value the quality of their relationships much more than their other accomplishments.

Lori, a forty-two-year-old freelance writer, still remembers the thing she hated most as a girl was "not being on good terms with my girlfriends."

"GO TO SLEEP, GIRLS!"

Slumber parties were the highlight of my social life as a little girl. A 1998 survey conducted by *All About You* magazine found that 96 per cent of girls younger than eighteen had dodged a pillow or two at a slumber party.

I saw them as a chance to test-drive my inner bad girl—staying up all night, eating junk food, playing practical jokes, making crank calls, and talking about boys incessantly.

Who can forget Truth or Dare, ouija boards, food/pillow/shaving cream/water balloon fights, having to go to the bathroom a zillion times during the course of the night? Inevitably, at some point, a fight would break out and someone would stomp off in tears.

And there was always one girl who actually wanted to sleep.

Child development specialist Penny Warner, author of *Slumber Parties: 25 Fun-Filled Party Themes*, says they are like a rite of passage that bonds little girls. "This is one of their first tastes of independence," says Warner. "They choose when to go to bed, what to do all night, and whom to include."

"I loved slumber parties," says Lori. "Even when they'd have this edge of hysteria to them, or maybe be- cause of that edge of hysteria. As we started to get close to puberty, sexuality entered the picture. I remember us creating a game that involved having to look at one anothers' bums or breasts (such as they were). There was also a striptease at that particular party."

For girls, a slumber party is an opportunity to spend time together and let their hair down, so to speak, without having parents or boys around. "The length of the party—overnight—gives them time to unwind, get comfortable, and get personal," says Warner. "It's like being on a deserted island with friends for a short period of time—a world unto its own."

Our Little Girl's a Woman Now

Nothing kicks the little girl out of you like the moment you see that first brown splotch on your undies.

One fine Saturday afternoon, you're eleven-year-old Donna, jumping up and down on the bed like the other kids, and the next thing you know, you go the bathroom and find a quarter-sized bloodstain on your underwear.

"I stared at it a long time, wondering how I could have hurt myself," Donna, now in her forties, remembers. "When I figured out what it was, I sent my cousins home and went to bed. It was four in the afternoon, but I felt like I needed to lie down. My mother and sister laughed uproariously when they found me in bed, lying down because I was 'sick.'" Donna had been given a booklet so she knew what was happening, but her overriding thought was Oh no! There's no going back now. This is it.

"Our baby's a woman now," Lori remembers her mother telling her father. "I was so embarrassed—I didn't want my father to know about my body."

We don't make nearly the same fuss when a boy has his first wet dream. Mom or Dad don't waltz out with his stained sheets and announce, "Look, honey, our boy is a man now!"

Yet doing research for this book, I was struck by the absolute glut of information on the subject of girls becoming women. Oddly enough, for all that has been said about this complex time, the experience itself is still so cloaked in Secret Language that it might as well come with its own dictionary.

Sadly, all I got was a little purple book that my mother discreetly pressed into my hand when I was twelve. It was called "Once a Month, the Egg Travels." I remember being confused. Where exactly did this mysterious egg travel—to the Bahamas? Was I meant to pack a bag for it, or what? I still wasn't quite clear on the whole egg/period/sex connection.

Nine-year-old Natalie burst into tears when her twelve-year-old sister, Christina, told her that getting her period meant she could have a baby. "I misunderstood and thought she meant I was going to have a baby," recalls Natalie, now a thirty-four-year-old English teacher. "I felt much too young to have a baby."

When Christina told another friend of hers one day that she was going to start bleeding through the same place she peed, her friend didn't believe her. "She turned white, went outside, and threw up," recalls Christina, now forty. "Apparently I forgot to tell her that it only lasts a few days at a time. She thought she was going to bleed constantly for the rest of her life."

And this was progress compared to what Christina's own mother went through as a young girl. Her mother grew up in the 1940s in a poor family and had to wear hand-me-down overalls that were too small. The straps cut into her so sharply that her shoulders bled. When she told her mother she thought she had got her period, she was hauled off to the doctor to have things explained, a common practice at the time. The doctor checked her out and told her that she did not, in fact, have her period. Christina's mom couldn't figure out why he was looking "down there" and pointed to her shoulders: "No it's here," she whispered.

I mean, ignorance may be bliss, but really, now.

Much of the secrecy and embarrassment surrounding our periods comes from the fact that menstruation isn't just about bleeding, it's the sign that a girl is growing up and becoming, gulp, a sexual being. Twenty-nine-year-old Krissandra thought she was dying when she first got her period as a teenager. In a way, part of her was.

"I think I realized that in a sense I was losing something: innocence, naiveté. It separated me from the girls who didn't have their periods, and my male friends suddenly saw me differently."

And while Mom and Dad may proudly announce that their baby is a woman now, it quickly becomes clear that that's about as much as anybody wants to hear.

THE MYTHS OF LIFE

- From the eighth to the eleventh centuries, churches refused Communion to menstruating women.
- Some African tribes believed that menstrual blood kept in a covered pot for nine months had the power to turn itself into a baby.
- Post-menopausal women were often the wisest because they retained their "wise blood." In the seventeenth century, these old women were constantly persecuted for witchcraft because it was thought that their menstrual blood remained in their veins.
- There was fear surrounding what early menarche symbolized. Some parents, even some doctors, tried to stop the process by restricting a girl's intake of foods considered to be sexually stimulating, such as cloves, pickles, and meat.
- According to Victorian medicine, the ovaries—not the brain—were the most important organ in the woman's body.
- Some have claimed that city girls enter puberty before country girls—and that brunettes menstruate before blondes—and many subscribed to the view that both black and Jewish girls menstruated early because they hailed originally from warm climates where sexuality was likely to be more primitive and precocious.

Our "Special Friend"

According to one study, 85 per cent of teenage girls feel it is "inappropriate to discuss menstruation with boys."

"It's her special friend," we whisper in mixed company when someone asks why so-and-so is doubled over with cramps in the corner. For something that was supposed to be our friend, it sure didn't seem very friendly.

"My friends and I had code words for it, like Aunt Flo," says Jennifer Lynn, a twenty-five-year-old freelance writer. "For emergencies, we asked if our friends had any 'girl stuff.'" Talk about a Secret Language!

I can still hear Chris Grela taunting me on the schoolbus when I was eleven: "What's a Kotex, Josey? You don't know, do you?" As much as I tried to fake it, I didn't know. All I knew was that there was a big blue box of this mysterious product under the bathroom counter at home that I was told was for older women.

It was all so clandestine. In fact, Tricia Warden writes about how getting her period made her feel like a secret spy in an essay in *The Bust Guide to the New Girl World Order*. "My mother told me when I got my period that I was to tell no one except her," writes Warden. "I was forbidden to bring up the subject if men or boys were present because I was told it was an extremely private thing. To give it that certain neurotic paranoid afraid-of-your-own-sexuality flair she gave it a code name. I felt like an agent of espionage. The code name was Rosy. In this way I could communicate with my mother if others, especially males, were present."

While magazines such as the *Ladies' Home Journal* and *Good Housekeeping* were running ads for Kotex as early as the 1920s, these mysterious feminine products could not be advertised on TV until the 1970s. And even then, who could tell what the hell those billowy ads featuring women in white pouring blue liquid on strips of cloth were all about?

Back in the 1950s, Kotex used slogans like "The right product gets the guy!" and "How humiliating if he discovers she is menstruating!" which had more to do with shame than reproduction.

Getting our periods was not about sexual development but about keeping our secret hidden and our bodies under control so that we could be popular. Today, the sanitary products (or even more cryptically, the "feminine hygiene") industry has built a more than $2-billion-a-year business on the premise that we can wear white jeans and go horseback riding without anyone ever knowing we're bleeding.

According to Joan Jacobs Brumberg, author of *The Body Project: An Intimate History of American Girls*, girls today have come to see their periods as a "hygienic crisis rather than as a maturational event. When they start menstruating, modern girls routinely reach for a sanitary napkin even before they reach for their mothers."

Not that we necessarily know what to do with one when we reach for it. "My mom used to throw away the instructions in the tampon box so the first two times I tried, I didn't know the cardboard thing was an applicator," thirty-one-year-old Jenny remembers. "I'd last about twenty minutes with it inside me before I had to take it out. I figured I was just not built for it."

Instructions didn't necessarily make things any clearer. "I figured out how to use tampons on my own," says Cathy, a twenty-eight-year-old nurse who grew up in a traditional Italian-American household. "But it took hours of sitting in my room trying to decipher those damn Tampax drawings and trying to figure out how they corresponded to my own body. I was afraid to ask my mom, because I thought using tampons was something bad, like virgins couldn't use them."

Jackie, a thirty-three-year-old office administrator, re-members her mother getting angry when she found out that Jackie was using tampons. "She told me they were for 'mar-ried women.'"

My mom had had a hysterectomy by the time I got my period, so she sent me to my sister for supplies. She handed me a super-size tampon and left the room. I still remember managing to get it in about halfway and spending the rest of the night shuffling around uncomfortably, feeling as if I had a cork stuck inside me.

I eventually figured out how to use tampons properly but was too embarrassed to ask my mother to buy them for me, so I walked two miles to the nearest store (we lived in the country) and prayed that the owner of the corner store didn't recognize me.

PERIOD CODE:
A ROSY BY ANY OTHER NAME

Here are some of the fabulous code names that have surfaced through the years for our periods. (I'm sure no one knows what you're talking about when you mention that your "snatch box is decorated with red roses" in mixed company.)

How a girl gets anything done with all those people dropping by . . .

- **Our friend**
- **Various relatives: Aunt Martha, Aunt Flo, Aunt Ruby, Aunt Tilly, my red-headed cousin, my red-headed aunt, Grandma, Cousin Tom (as in "Time Of the Month")**
- **The Cardinal**
- **The French lady**
- **Lady in the red dress**
- **Monthly monster**

It's enough to make you sick . . .

- **The Plague**
- **Broken**
- **Under the weather**
- **Closed for maintenance**

- **The Curse**
- **My Sick Time**

You can't blame us for seeing red . . .
- **The hunt for red October**
- **Riding the red ball special**
- **Riding the red tide**
- **The red-letter day**
- **The reds are in**
- **The red flag is up**

And in the just plain disturbing category . . .
- **Monthly evacuations**
- **Riding the cotton pony**
- **It's raining down south**
- **I've got my flowers**
- **On the rag**
- **Riding the cycle**
- **Bloody Mary**
- **Tide's in**
- **Too wet to plow**
- **A snatch box decorated with red roses**
- **Weeping womb**
- **My pussycat has a nosebleed**
- **White cylinder week**
- **Jam and bread**

A Secret Society

While I may have been embarrassed to talk to Mom about it, I couldn't wait to tell my friends. I'll never forget how much it annoyed me that as I was the tomboy in my group of friends, it was assumed I would get my period last. Imagine my joy the day I discovered my brown splotch as I was sitting in the stall of the school bathroom. Instinctively, I packed a wad of rough toilet paper—the nasty kind that comes in those little folded individual squares—into my undies and smugly headed back to class. I could hardly wait for recess to share my news with the group.

As soon as the four of us were assembled in our usual huddle in our corner of the yard, I blurted out, "I got it!" as if I had just won the lottery. The response was mixed. Kelli, the first in our group to get her period (she already had boobs and hips in Grade 7), seemed genuinely happy for me. "Oh, my God!" she cried with appropriate enthusiasm. The other two held back. I remember being disappointed that they weren't more excited for me. I'd obviously already forgotten what it was like to feel outside the club.

The only thing worse than losing your childhood to puberty is being left behind in childhood while your friends mature. "I was a late bloomer in all aspects," says twenty-eight-year-old Lesa, an assistant fashion magazine editor, "whether it was getting my period, getting boobs (and then having them be tiny as hell), or having a boyfriend and losing my virginity, I always seemed to be last and I hated it."

The Body Project author Brumberg blames the sanitary product industry at least in part for turning menstruation into more of a social than a biological event. Part of their strategy, she believes, was to literally take Mom out of the picture. According to Brumberg, by the time the Second World War ended, mothers started to disappear from ads altogether and companies began to market their products to teenage girls directly.

And true enough, as early as the forties, Kotex put out booklets like the one I found at the Museum of Menstruation (I kid you not—check it out at www.mum.com) titled "As One Girl to Another," explaining menstruation. Similar booklets throughout the fifties, sixties, and seventies depict girls walking arm in arm, hanging out together. The implied message was that menstruation was an experience you share with your girlfriends, not your mother.

Certainly, many of the women I spoke to didn't want Mom involved. "When I was twelve or thirteen, my mother attempted to fill me in, but I told her I already knew all about it. I was really uncomfortable with the idea of my mother telling me this stuff," says thirty-seven-year-old Karen, who adds that she learned more about menstruation from girls at school than from home. But I'm not sure we can blame Kotex entirely for our need to turn away from Mom at this point. While Mom may be our "girl guide" until this point,

BLEEDING ACROSS CULTURES

Not everyone gets as squeamish about menses as we Westerners. In some cultures, a girl's getting her period is cause for celebration!

Korea
A girl may be given a dinner in her honour when she has her first period. One of the traditional dishes for this occasion is a special soup made of seaweed.

Melville Island
Among the Tiwi people of Melville Island, a girl having her first menstrual period leaves the general community and goes out into the wild with other women to set up a new camp.

Australia
In some ceremonies, Aboriginal men cut themselves to imitate women's menstruation. In some tribes, men cut open their penises to reproduce the look of a bleeding vulva.

India
When a Nayar girl of India begins her period, she may be secluded and visited by neighbouring women

and dressed in new clothes. She will usually start wearing a sari, a woman's dress, at this time. Later, she and her friends will take a ceremonial bath, and then go to a feast where drums are beaten and shouts of joy are made.

Uganda

When a girl gets her first period, she may stay home from school. Her mother and aunts will spend the day with her and tell her things she needs to know. Later, her girlfriends come to visit and have a party during which they sing a song about menstruation to celebrate.

puberty is our first real opportunity to explore womanhood on our own terms, separate from Mom.

Instead of turning to Mom, we tend to seek out others going through the same thing. Remember Judy Blume's puberty classic, *Are You There God? It's Me, Margaret*? Our library copy was dog-eared and worn from use. As young girls, we identified so strongly with young Margaret's experience, and the anxiety, excitement, and anticipation of all the changes that were (or weren't) happening to us. The fact that Margaret and her friends form a secret club to mark their various milestones together—getting breasts, kissing boys, wishing for their periods—reflected our own need and desire to be part of a club.

In this exciting, scary new world, we need others who understand exactly what we're going through. To give us knowing, sympathetic looks when we're sitting on the sidelines during gym class. To be versed in the Secret Language so that when we whisper "spot check," they know to immediately fall a few steps behind us and check for leaks. Or if we whisper, "pad check," they'll check whether the bulky outline of a pad is visible through our tight jeans.

In Training?

While menstruation is our dirty little secret, boobs enjoy no such cover. Breasts are the first visible (or, for some of us, not so visible) sign of puberty. Suddenly, without any of our own doing, we make a sexual statement every time we walk into a room.

"I got mine late and they were bigger than most," says Jennifer, a twenty-three-year-old fundraiser for a women's non-profit organization. "I hated being the only girl with no breasts, but as soon as I got them, I hated that even more. All of a sudden, boys were staring at my chest, and girls I did not even know glared at me with contempt." Suddenly, assumptions about us are made based on the size of our breasts. Like, obviously the Grade 7 girl with tits whom my boyfriend dumped me for was a slut.

Like getting your period, a confusing mix of desire and resentment surrounds boobs. And just as sanitary products can be seen as both a sign of sexual maturity and of keeping sexual maturity under control, your first bra is another experience often tinged with embarrassment, excitement, and plenty of secrecy.

Lori remembers her mother insisting on taking her shopping for a training bra when she was eleven. "I was so embarrassed in the store—I didn't want to admit that my body was changing. I still felt like a kid."

I was in Grade 9 when my best friend boldly suggested I start wearing a bra. I felt so clueless as I looked down at the budding protrusions under my T-shirt. In a particularly sweet Secret Language moment, my friend lent me one of her bras. It was a Dici. Remember those flimsy crossover ones with the frontal closure? I was too embarrassed to tell my mom. I hoped she wouldn't notice. After that, I snuck my sister's bras until I was brave enough to buy my own. Once again, I felt like I was in the club. That took away some of the embarrassment.

In a study on adolescents and bras by Merewyn Hines, a University of Toronto student, one of the participants remembers the thrill of her first bra. Given to her by a friend, the bra was worn under layers of clothes during weekly horseback riding lessons, even though the young girl was almost completely flat. "It used to make me so happy knowing I had a secret, that I was wearing a *bra*," she recalls.

Girls spend a lot of time talking about who does and doesn't wear a bra.

"It was soooo embarrassing being one of the first girls in the class to start wearing one," recalls another woman in

Hines's study. "One of my friends got one around the same time I did, and she wore two tight undershirts over it so that the bra line wouldn't be obvious through her shirt. I copied her and did the same thing, but some of the jokers in my class still managed to sneak up and snap it."

Interestingly, bras weren't even marketed to teenage girls until the fifties, Brumberg writes in *The Body Project*. Before that, girls wore undershirts until they could fit into adult bras. Companies such as Warners, Maidenform, Formfit, Belle Mode, and Perfect Form (as well as popular magazines like *Good Housekeeping*) started the notion of "junior figure control" and encouraged the idea that young women needed both lightweight girdles and bras to "start the figure off to a beautiful future."

This was really just a marketing ploy to sell bras to teenagers. I mean, think about it. What are training bras about really? What, are my AAA boobs gonna run a marathon? As a bra saleswoman once told me, "Training bras are not training anything." Before you knew it, says Brumberg, girls everywhere start worrying about who did and who didn't wear a bra. "The ability to wear and fill a bra was central to an adolescent girl's status and sense of self," she writes.

"I have little boobs, and though I love them now, I used to feel so inadequate," says Jesse, a twenty-one-year-old student. "Once I went to school with a Wonderbra on, and I guess it was obvious that my boobs had never been that big before. Some boy asked my friend what had happened to me, and I was so embarrassed I threw the bra out as soon as I got home."

Brumberg believes the introduction of mass-produced bras for young girls also contributed to making us feel like freaks if they didn't fit us. "Suddenly, the body had to fit into standard sizes that were constructed from a pattern representing a norm. When clothing failed to fit the body, particularly a part as intimate as the breasts, young women were apt to perceive that there was something wrong with their bodies making them self-conscious about their breasts."

Christina remembers getting into a huge fight with her mother while shopping for her first bra. She kept insisting that she needed an AAA while her mother wanted to buy her an A-cup bra. "I assumed that AAA was bigger than A simply because there were more A's," she recalls. "When the saleslady asked me if I realized that AAA was smaller than A, she and my mom had a good laugh at my expense. I was absolutely mortified."

Don't even get me started on the Secret Language of bra sizes. There are plenty of grown women who don't even understand that.

Our Bodies, Our Self-Consciousness

With so many changes happening to our bodies, we naturally feel a little self-conscious. According to Brumberg, even Simone de Beauvoir stressed out about her changing body. Back in the 1920s, the feminist writer and philosopher wrote that at fifteen she looked simply "awful." She had acne, her clothes no longer fitted, and she had to wrap her breasts in bandages because her favourite beige silk party dress pulled so tightly across her new bosom that it looked "obscene."

"Just as pregnant women focus on their bodies, so adolescent girls focus on their changing bodies," writes Mary Pipher in *Reviving Ophelia: Saving the Selves of Adolescent Girls*. "At thirteen, I thought more about my acne than I did about God or world peace. At thirteen, many girls spend more time in front of a mirror than they do on their studies. Small flaws become obsessions. Bad hair can ruin a day. A broken fingernail can feel tragic."

Girls who develop early seem to get hit the hardest. "I was the first of my classmates to get hips and tits, and I always felt like a big conspicuous fatty," Roxanne, a twenty-two-year-old bookstore clerk, recalls. Looking back now, Roxanne realizes that she wasn't really fat at all, just "the fattest compared to all the skinny girls, who to me reflected the population of the world."

And it can be a cruel world. Sara, a twenty-four-year-old communications assistant and freelance writer, was an active girl, who, like many girls, gained weight during puberty and became known as "the fat girl" or, as her stepsister called her, Fatso. When she went to summer camp one year, a group of girls she assumed were her friends sent her fake secret admirer notes—complete with, if you can believe it, candy —and even encouraged her to meet the admirer. He never showed up, of course.

This feeling that we're not good enough, that we don't measure up—not to mention going to extremes to make ourselves attractive—has long been a theme in the lives of teenage girls.

In the adolescent diaries that she studied, Brumberg observed that it wasn't until the 1920s that girls started writing about "intimate interactions with boys at parties, in cars, and at the movies." They also began to write about using clothing and makeup to be sexually attractive and "for the first time, they tried 'slimming,' a new body project tied to the scientific discovery of the calorie."

Consider these two quotes, penned ninety years apart. In 1892, one girl wrote: "Resolved not to talk about myself or feelings. To think before speaking. To work seriously. To be self-restrained in conversation and actions. Not to let my thoughts wander. To be dignified. Interest myself more in others." A New Year's resolution from 1982 read: "I will try to make myself better in any way I possibly can with the help of my budget and baby-sitting money. I will lose weight, get new lenses; already got new haircut, good makeup, new clothes and accessories." Since the sixties, across class and race, diary entries have consistently included statements like "I've got to lose weight," and "I must starve myself."

A recent Canadian Teachers' Federation Report said that 85 per cent of teenage girls worry "a lot" about how they look. The study showed that 74 per cent of teenage girls between fifteen and nineteen years of age would like to lose weight and feel that looking good, much of which is measured by their weight, is important to attracting boyfriends. "Dieting, exercise and the self-policing of their bodies is a pervasive part of the collective engagement that girls have with each other," writes Liz Frost in *Young Women and the Body: A Feminine Sociology*. "It is part of the language and activity of girl culture." If you think about it, it makes sense. At a time when your body is changing in ways you can't control, and people are reacting to it in ways you can't control, intake of food is one thing you can control. And since we're all in the same boat, dieting creates another personal body struggle to bond over.

Kim Chernin, an American author who has written many books on eating disorders and the culture of dieting, has observed dieting as a form of bonding in groups of young women. "It is part of the group identification process centred on a culture of calorie counting, exercise and other aspects of body control that becomes central to the reinforcement of group belonging."

Group Mentality

God knows, it's all about belonging when you're a teenage girl. If you think being part of the group is important for girls on the playground, it becomes a way of life during the tumultuous teenage years. We need each other to get through these crazy changes and to figure out who we are as young women.

While little girls overwhelmingly turn to Mom for advice, according to the smartgirl.com survey I mentioned last chapter, by age twelve, 77 per cent of girls turn to friends instead. "I have a good relationship with my mom," says twenty-year-old Cori, a nursing student whose mother was only a teenager when she had her. "But for some things, I go to my girlfriends first so I can get an opinion before going to Mom and Dad."

"[As teens], peer groups have more influence than parents," says Myrna Kostash, author of *No Kidding: Inside the World of Teenage Girls.*

"My best friend for most of high school was Monique," says Jenny, a thirty-one-year-old graduate student. "We got into all of our trouble together, like shoplifting and drinking. We talked on the phone constantly and hung out every weekend. We even binged and purged together."

And unlike boys, who, according to Cori, are always interrupting and thinking they have all the answers, girls offer "a shoulder to cry on and are more likely to sit and listen." Girls are even more physically intimate, she says. "Guys will sit at opposite ends of a couch and girls will sit right beside each other," she tells me. I recently walked by a mall and saw several teenage girls sprawled out on the sidewalk out front, their bodies tangled together, talking and laughing. I often see teenage girls walking arm in arm or holding hands. It's impossible to imagine teenage boys doing the same.

Bedroom Culture

One of my favourite activities as a teenager was hanging out in a girlfriend's bedroom, making crank phone calls, gossiping about boys and other girls at school, trying on each others' clothes, and complaining about our parents. I loved that warm fun secret world, the sheer joy of knowing your friends were close, physically and emotionally. They got you. Nothing needed explaining. You shared the Secret Language, and your bedroom was like a secret clubhouse.

Despite all the wretched stuff going on in our lives, nothing bad could ever happen in this wonderful bubble we created. We were allies, a united front, safe with each other in our bedrooms with our stuff, our music, and our posters of teen idols Sean Cassidy and Willie Ames. Today, the posters might be of Justin Timberlake, but the effect is the same.

Pop culture theorists Angela McRobbie and Jenny Garber actually coined the term "culture of the bedroom" in the seventies. Boys, they argue, dominate the streets, while girls hang out in their bedrooms and do what teenage girls do—read magazines, listen to music, dance, and talk about boys, fashion, and who likes whom. And while girls feel the pressure to learn what it takes to be "feminine" and "beautiful" in order to attract boys, learning this stuff with other girls is fun. Sure, some of it fosters insecurity and reinforces expectations of beauty, but there is also a sense of power to be had from getting good at doing "attractive." One woman I spoke with fondly remembers this: "It was a wonderful time when I first began getting attention from boys," says twenty-eight-year-old Kathy, who works at a publishing firm. "My friends and I spent hours talking about clothes, experimenting with makeup and going places where we knew we'd see boys. My relationships with those girls were my favourite relationships. I'm always trying to get that feeling back."

Girl Talk

Even by this age, girls have learned the value of talking to each other, with most teenage girls describing their favourite thing to do together as "talking." Actually, what most of them say is "We like to sit around and 'just' talk," notes Vivienne Griffiths in *Adolescent Girls and Their Friends: A Feminist Ethnography*. The girls sound almost apologetic and critical of the activity, as though they feel they should be doing something considered more productive.

By this age, we have already learned to undervalue our own talk. This attitude is reinforced by the critical view taken of girls' talk in school, says Griffiths. "Like laughing, talking was one of the most frequently reprimanded aspects of girls' behaviour in class, and seen as an aspect of teenage girls' general silliness in comparison to boys," she writes. "Such criticisms of girls' talk are not isolated incidents, but part of a wider devaluation of talk between women which many feminist researchers have identified." As someone who was constantly getting in trouble for talking in class, I'm all over this one.

Griffiths noticed that even in her own field research notes, she often referred to girls "chatting" or "chattering" together, whereas the boys are always described as "talking." She also noted that while girls usually described the act of talking together in positive terms, they often referred to their talking as "nattering," "gossiping," or "bitching."

Mind you, as it has been throughout history, negative attitudes about female talk don't shut us up or make us need or love to talk any less. Talking is too important to us. Besides, we're good at it. Like guys who grow up shooting hoops with each other and develop a "natural" talent for basketball, girls who spend all their time talking together become pretty skilled yakkers.

"Friends coach each other to talk," write Terri Apter and Ruthellen Josselson in *Best Friends: The Pleasures and Perils of Girls' and Women's Friendships*. The authors describe how young women, without being fully being aware of it, learn "to listen each other into speech." We may go to a friend unsure of what we need to express. But by talking, and having her listen, our girlfriend makes a space for us to try to express ourselves verbally. "This capacity to listen empathetically, to pick up and shape ideas together, is not simply inbred," write Apter and Josselson. "Rather, it is a talent constantly honed in the world of girls' and women's friendships."

Teenage girls need to talk things through to make sense of the world around them. They also need to hear that they are not alone. "Oh my God, me too!" is one of the most common phrases uttered between teenage girls. It communicates a shared understanding and a shared experience. It makes you feel like less of a freak.

In *ManifestA*, Jennifer Baumgardner and Amy Richards talk about the popularity of teen magazine sections like *Seventeen*'s "Trauma-rama," which encourage readers to write in with absurd tales of bodily dysfunction and embarrassment. "For example, one girl wrote in about standing in a store when her bloody pad fell onto her shoe just as a cute boy—a hottie—walked in. Other tales include accidentally farting in class, bleeding through a pink skirt, and having a boyfriend diss a girlfriend for her halitosis." The authors believe these sections are popular "because girls really want to know that they aren't alone: the confidences come from the girls themselves, rather than from the adult editors and writers, and are meant for other girls who are dealing with body hair and smells and sex for the first time—just like them." These common experiences give girls a wonderfully comforting identification.

"Teens who hardly speak to their parents talk all night with friends," according to Mary Pipher in *Reviving Ophelia*. "Peers validate their decisions and support their new independent selves. This is a time of deep searching for the self in relationships. There is a constant experimenting—what reaction will I get from others? Talking to friends is a way of checking the important question—Am I okay?"

Girls also need to confide in other girls. Although girls may learn the "facts" from adult women (often their mothers),

DEAR DIARY

Keep a diary and someday it'll keep you. – Mae West

Know many boys who kept a diary? If they did, they more likely called it a journal. Many women I spoke to admitted that while they may have kept a diary as a teen, they now prefer to call it a journal.

The diary, like most things strictly associated with female communication, is seen as trivial. We imagine the silly scribblings of young girls under lock and key. But diaries were once one of the few outlets for women's writings.

According to Valerie Raoul in *Women and Diaries: Gender and Genre*, nineteenth-century women were discouraged from writing for the public. However, the diary, because it was a private, non-literary form of writing, was considered an acceptable forum for women's writing. "Non-productive private writing was allowed as an accomplishment and recreation as long as it did not interfere with the business of being of a woman," writes Raoul. "A woman's business was to stay away from business, including writing as a marketable skill."

Diaries became an outlet for expression at a time when silence was considered to be a female virtue.

According to Suzanne L. Bunkers, author of "Faithful Friends: Diaries and the Dynamics of Women's Friendships" in the book *Communication and Women's Friendships*, the diary took on the role of a beloved sister or a constant, faithful friend. "Dear Diary" is a direct address to an ideal audience: always available, always listening, and always sympathetic.

Many women told me that their diaries were especially important during the teenage years when fitting in and feeling judged by peers can be overwhelming. Their diary was a friend to confide in without fear or criticism.

Diaries often focus on the details and minutiae of daily life, something that has been historically associated with domestic life and women.

Details and minutiae were what I was all about when it came to the diary I kept faithfully from age thirteen to fourteen. It was filled with page after page about what boy I liked that week or what girlfriend was making me crazy, complete with blow-by-blow accounts of monumental events like first kisses or being asked to dance by someone I liked. Monique, a twenty-four-year-old journalism student, says that many a page in her diary was dedicated to "self-pity for not being invited to the 'cool kids' party or not being asked out by the right boy."

they need one another to explore and work out the tangled set of emotions that arise as they become sexual beings. They need to talk about their bodies, their desires, and their anxieties and guilts. No way are you talking to boys or Mom about that stuff. You know that if you tell Mom you like a guy she's going to immediately get all protective and worry about how far the two of you have gone or what his intentions are. Unlike with your girlfriends, you can't just talk to her about how you feel about things. Boys, on the other hand, just don't get it. Nope, the only place your secrets are safe are with your girlfriends. Which is why so many girls say the worst thing a girlfriend can do is betray a confidence by telling someone else your secrets.

Playing Cool

Unfortunately, at a time when best friends become more and more crucial, the alliance-forming habits of the playground combined with the insecurities of puberty can also turn teenage girls into the most loathsome creatures on the planet. Although most of the women I talked to revelled in the joys of female friendships and waxed poetic about the support and love they get from other women, few had quite the same warm, fuzzy feelings for the treacherous teenage years.

If Mom's our first teacher of how to "do" girl, the teenage years are when other girls decide if we're doing girl right.

Whether that means having the right clothes or the right friends, teenage girls are brutal when it comes to judging what is acceptable and what is not.

The pressure to fit in during puberty is enormous for girls. *Seventeen* magazine capitalized on (and no doubt perpetuated) this way back in 1944 when they launched Teena, a prototypical teenage girl created by the magazine's editors. According to contributor Kelly Schrum in the book *Delinquents and Debutantes: Twentieth-Century American Girls' Cultures*, the magazine used the slogan "Teena is a copycat—what a break for you! . . . She and her teen-mates speak the same language . . . wear the same clothes . . . use the same brand of lipstick." We don't all get such a break, and trying to fit in can seem impossible at times.

When Kimberly, a twenty-nine-year-old assistant editor, was growing up, a certain brand of designer jeans was really in. Her family was poor and couldn't afford them. When she finally got a pair of Jordache jeans for her birthday, she wore them "until I'd worn creases in the legs and bare patches in the knees and butt." She also got grief for trying to fit in by feathering her wild and curly hair. "One of my friends told me I looked like I had sausages all over my head." Experimenting with makeup was equally disastrous. "There are a few really hideous pictures of me with huge, totally natural eyebrows and peacock blue eye shadow," Kimberly recalls. "I also had buckteeth before I got braces, so the effect was really horrific. I remember throwing a fit one time because my family was ready to go somewhere, and I wasn't ready, so they all had to wait while I applied my makeup, sort of crying at the same time. I was so misunderstood."

"The teenage years are the time when you start picking out your own clothes," recalls Paula, a thirty-six-year-old Web designer. "And you need money to fit in because the rich girls set the fashion scene and everyone else is expected to follow; otherwise, you face utter humiliation with your imitation CK jeans!"

Sometimes even the right jeans can't help. "It's hard to fit in to a blond-haired, blue-eyed Minnesota Catholic school when your dad's from India," say Sheela, a twenty-five-year-old musician.

Anne, a twenty-seven-year-old librarian remembers the pressure of having to live up to certain standards. "We looked up to the Solid Gold Dancers, Olivia Newton-John, Daisy Duke, and the women of Abba as examples of physical beauty," she recalls. "We thought you needed to develop large breasts to be beautiful and that we should wear clothes that accented our female shape in order to gain respect."

Whether it's Olivia or Britney, the song remains the same. In *Reviving Ophelia*, Mary Pipher writes about the conformist impulse in girls. "Many girls become good haters of those who do not conform sufficiently to our culture's ideas about femininity. They rush to set standards in order to ward off the imposition of others' standards on them."

The content of the standards is variable—designer jeans

or leather jackets, smoking cigarettes, or the heavy use of eye shadow. The underlying message—that not fitting in is social suicide—is not, according to Pipher.

Some girls said they would do almost anything to fit in. Take Nancy, a twenty-eight-year-old law student. When Debbie and Donna, the cool girls that everyone longed to be friends with, decided they wanted Nancy to be their friend, Nancy desperately tried to live up to her newfound status. "I sat and talked to them about clothes, makeup, nail polish, and all that stuff until I was blue," she tells me. "Don't get me wrong; I love talking about all that stuff, but not *just* that stuff. I was going crazy. This was not what being liked was supposed to be about. But there was no one else jumping up to be my friend, so I stuck it out."

When Liz, a thirty-year-old graduate student, was in Grade 7, she was part of the "in" crowd even though they forbade her to talk to her old friends from Grade 6. They wore the same clothes on specified days. "I even got pink eye when we all purposefully shared the eyeliner of someone who had pink eye," she says, laughing.

Even if you're not part of the popular crowd, the need to find somewhere to belong is tremendous. "I got along better with girls once I reached high school, because I was lucky enough to fall in with a crowd of outcasts—girls who, like me, hadn't fit in before," says Jenny, who is in her late twenties. "We formed our own clique of outcasts, disdained by the 'preppies.'"

She's a Slut!

It's one thing to compare yourself with other girls in order to feel like you're less of a freak, but it's another to slag other girls in order to make yourself feel normal. But teenage girls do this all the time (yes, we big girls do it too, but more on that later).

At this point, fear, anger, and disappointment fuel our communication and our language is not only secret, it's downright sneaky. On one hand, teenage girls will innocently gossip about one anothers' lives in order to see how their own measure up. We want to know what other girl's lives are like, what problems they have, and who they are, as opposed to who they seem to be.

But teenage girls also use gossip to ostracize girls who are different or whom they feel threatened by. This can get rather nasty and unsisterly, indeed. "'She's always showing off,' 'She's weird,' 'She flirts like a slut' are all judgments that make use of the norms girls construct together," say Terri Apter and Ruthellen Josselson in *Best Friends*. Much of this need to put others in their place no doubt arises from the insecurities girls feel about their own physical and sexual selves. At the same time, the verbal nature of this viciousness can be attributed to the way girls are taught to express anger.

Girls do not express their anger directly, says *Reviving Ophelia* author Mary Pipher. Unlike boys, girls do not learn to fight physically with their enemies. Instead, girls use cattiness and teasing. They'll punish another girl by phoning to say that there's a party and she's not invited or insulting another girl's clothes or body. Or by using nicknames and derogatory labels. "They pass along damaging and probably spurious tales about each other's sexual behaviour and reputation calling other girls slut, bitch, sleaze," write Apter and Josselson. "They cruelly disparage each other's bodies— so-and-so's tits hang down to here, man, and so-and-so's thighs are gross, and check out that hairdo—what a rat's nest.'"

And just as they learned on the schoolyard, rather than directly kick someone out of the group, girls work through alliances. If they feel alliances shifting, they make a preemptive strike to exclude someone else so as not to be excluded themselves. "They may want to strengthen their position by getting others on their side as they cast someone out," write Apter and Josselson. "These cruel experiments of inclusion and exclusion form the basis of the clique."

I remember at age twelve "dropping" my best friend on a Monday morning after I had spent the weekend with another girl I'd decided was my new best friend. After that, switching alliances was a weekly occurrence during my teen years. We regularly reevaluated who was best friends with whom, who was on the outs, and who to bring into our group.

One girl described it as not being able to trust your friends fully, fearing that when your back is turned they will put you down, that something is being planned that you'll be excluded from, or that the others know something you don't. This is the vicious side to the intimacy and bond that girls create together. All the pressure to fit in, to be feminine but not too sexy, to win the attention of boys can pit girls against each other when competition kicks in.

"I went to an all-girl school in Saudi Arabia," twenty-eight-year-old Zahra tells me. "When I moved to Canada in Grade 8, I saw a difference in the relationships between girls because of the presence of boys—I saw competition and backstabbing." Zahra admits that girls can be extremely cruel and cliquey without boys, but throwing boys into the mix heightens things.

In an essay about board games for girls titled "Boys-R-Us: Board Games and the Socialization of Young Adolescent Girls," Jennifer Scanlon describes a game called Sweet Valley High in which girls race around the school trying to retrieve a boyfriend, a teacher chaperon, and all the accessories needed for a big date. In the process of trying to get it all done first, girls can steal other girls' boyfriends or fight over guys, and such behaviour receives rewards. "Girls play these games together," writes Scanlon, "but rather than promoting positive female culture or solidarity, the games teach girls that they cannot trust each other when it comes to their 'primary' life definition: boys."

Anne remembers the pressure to have a boyfriend. "Whenever we didn't have one, we found someone to have a crush on, no matter how unrealistic it might have been," she tells me. "Even though our group placed little overt value on boys, we all spent a lot of time focusing on them."

While we are curious about boys and sex, we have already had it drilled into us that being overt about it is not acceptable. Girls are supposed to be proper and any signs of sexuality are to be hidden. We may talk to each other about our secret desires, but publicly there is still a silence surrounding girls' sexual desire. "Rarely is there acknowledgment in movies or TV that sex is pleasurable for girls, just as it is for boys, and that girls have desire, just as boys do," writes Leora Tanenbaum in *Slut!: Growing Up Female with a Bad Reputation.* "Sex for boys is blissful according to popular culture, whereas for girls it has repercussions." Most of the information I see about girls and sex has to do with warning them about pregnancy or having sex too young. They are rarely told that sex might be something to enjoy or pursue for pleasure.

After combing through sex education literature and researching public school curricula, psychologist Michelle Fine found that young women are rarely depicted as autonomous sexual beings. They are instead portrayed as wanting sex only for the emotional intimacy and as utterly lacking in sex drive. The point conveyed is that "good" girls do not have sexual desires. If a girl does have sex, it's because she is pressured or coerced—or else she's a "slut." I am amazed at the endurance of this label.

More amazing is that a slut is not merely a girl who "does it," but any girl who—through her clothes, makeup, hairstyle, or speech—seems as if she might, writes Peggy Orenstein in

School Girls: Young Women, Self-Esteem, and the Confidence Gap. For example, when everyone else in the class is wearing training bras, the girl with developed breasts becomes an object of sexual scrutiny. When boys develop early, they are not similarly stigmatized.

Strangely, it's not necessarily the boys who label girls as sluts for their perceived or real behaviour; sometimes it's other girls. This is part of defining ourselves as sexual beings, says Orenstein. "Girls do not want to be seen as prudes or as sluts," she writes. "In order to find the middle ground between the two, a place from which they can function safely and with approval, girls have to monitor both their expressions of intelligence and their budding sexual desire. They must keep vigilant watch over each other and over themselves."

"There were many girls who got the unfortunate slut label without seeming exceptionally slutty," recalls Roxanne. "They just pissed off the wrong girls. Forget the 'male gaze'—it's the female gaze that determines your sluttiness when you are young."

Jenny agrees. "It was the girls who labelled other girls sluts," she tells me. "Teenage girls label everybody. When they are confronted with someone who doesn't fit their idea of how a girl should act or look, they grasp for an insulting label. Typically the girl with the 'slut' reputation fails to conform in some way. 'Slut' becomes an insult like any other, with sexual implications thrown in for added measure."

Both boys and girls can inflict emotional harm, but when girls are involved, the harassment tends to become more personal, says Tanenbaum. "If a girl gets a reputation and then does something that gets on another girl's nerves, that girl is going to immediately mention the reputation. Like, 'Not only did she do better than me on that test but she's also a slut.'"

Tired of this old label, one woman I spoke to has given the word new meaning. "If I were to use it in a sexual way, it would mean someone who sleeps with whomever they want—a woman who does what she wants, instead of what she's 'supposed' to—and it would be a compliment rather than an insult." She and her friends started a SLUTS club in which she and her other single girlfriends turned the label into an acronym for "Still Lovely Unclaimed Treasures." Funnily enough, she says, none of them actually slept around much.

GOOD GIRLS DON'T: MIXED MESSAGES

How's a gal supposed to feel good about her sexuality when we get these messages growing up?

Good girls wait until they are married, or at least in love. Only skanky girls do it for fun. – Jennifer, 23

It's not really appropriate in my [East Indian] culture to talk about these subjects openly so my mom didn't really talk to me. All she said to me was "Don't do it before you're married." – Sapna, 27

My mother said, "Always make yourself available to your husband so he doesn't go elsewhere."
— Stacey, 35

When I got to a certain age, I was told I could no longer go to a guy friend's house alone. "What would people think?" was the message. When I first came to Canada [from Saudi Arabia], I remember being shocked when someone spoke openly about sex in public. — Leila, 24

My mother always said "Keep your skirt down and your panties up." — Lyn, 34

Girls are generally not to be sexual beings, and sex is for procreation only. — Sheela, 25

Masturbation for girls was bad but tolerable for guys.
— Katherine, 26

I remember my mom telling me that the best present I could give my husband on my wedding day was my virginity. To her credit, I did stay a virgin until I was almost twenty-one. — Roxanne, 22

Girls should avoid sex until they're married; otherwise, they're sluts. One of my best friends got pregnant at sixteen and my parents wouldn't let me hang out with her as much any more because she was "bad."
— Sarah, 21

Me and the Girls

You'd think after what we put each other through as teenagers, women would swear off female friendships forever. Lynne, a twenty-seven-year-old television producer, says she pretty much wrote off girls after high school. "I didn't feel like I could trust them," she says. "But it's amazing how important girlfriends have become as I've gotten older. I've found some great women with fantastic outlooks on the world with whom I find a real camaraderie." Like war vets, only other women can understand the hell you've been through. We are drawn to each other. Our girlfriends remain our lifelines.

"They are my sanity, my crutches, my steadfast companions," says Roxanne, a twenty-two-year-old bookstore clerk and art history student, who also felt burned by girls in high school and had to learn to trust women again. "My girlfriends understand me better than any man ever could, and I know they will love me unconditionally and with more loyalty than any man ever will. We are kind of like *Sex and the City* girls, where the men come and go, but we are fiercely devoted to one another."

Men are often freaked out by how easily women open up to each other. By adulthood, the Secret Language is second nature. A girlfriend who doesn't give it up is viewed with suspicion. What's her problem?

We make sense of the world through our friendships. Just as "Me too" was our favourite phrase as teenagers, phrases like "Oh my God, I totally know what you mean," or "I had the same thing happen to me," are our way of making each other feel validated and normal.

"I get affirmation from my girlfriends," says twenty-three-year-old Tukiso, an international relations student. "If someone echoes what I'm feeling, even if it's not the exact experience I've had, it confirms I'm not crazy. Sometimes I think so many things are against me in the world—I'm female, I'm black—it's nice to know there's support out there."

We can let loose with the girls, laugh, express fears, ask for help. We can obsess about our love lives, our kids, our hair, our weight, our achievements. We can shop. We can cook. We can eat, drink, and laugh. We make life easier for each other. When we lose ourselves, our girlfriends know where to find us. Friendships are one place you can make yourself vulnerable. "I can tell my best friend things I wouldn't dare to tell my mother or even my psychiatrist," says Krista, a nineteen-year-old college student. When you know things about each other that no one else does, it's better than a blood pact. Violating this trust is unspeakable and punishable by removal of friendship privileges.

As Roxanne points out, girlfriends often know us better than lovers do. They accept us more readily. They usually don't leave at the first sign of trouble. Unlike relationships that come and go, friendships endure, which is not to say that you can't break up with girlfriends. Just as in the schoolyard, alliances can shift. But they become less fickle. You don't stop hanging out with your girlfriend because she's not wearing the right kind of pants (we might convince her to go shopping with us for new ones, mind you).

Female friendships are messy and complicated. Sometimes your life sucks and hers is swimming along. Sometimes she's demanding and asking things of you that you would never ask of her. Sometimes we forget how important our friends are because we temporarily let boys get in the way.

In other words, there's always room for improvement.

"Generally, there's that trust and longevity," says twenty-seven-year-old Melanie, one half of Diva Productions, a company she started with a girlfriend in Toronto, which regularly holds girls' nights. "There's an understanding that I can tell a girlfriend the most horrible thing I've ever done and she's going to back me on it."

"My close friends know me like no one else," says Melany, a twenty-eight-year-old counsellor. "They know how impetuous I am, and how I tend to sell myself short. They know me better than my parents."

Girlfriends are your "nice" mirror. When a girlfriend asks if we think what she is doing is stupid, and we do, we don't tell her. At least not outright. We ask her why she thinks it's stupid and reassure her that, well hey, we've all done things we've regretted, and anyway she could never do anything truly stupid because we love her so much.

Men don't get this. They think that if you ask them something you want an honest answer. Really, all you're asking for is some reassurance that you're not a complete ass, no matter how much of an ass you're being. When you confess to your girlfriend that you spent the previous night in front of the TV instead of meeting a deadline, she'll tell you that you obviously needed a break. When your girlfriend tells you she was upset over something and managed to polish off half a carrot cake, you tell her that her body must have been craving beta carotene.

There are enough things in this world to make us feel bad. Girlfriends are a break from that. We need to know we can do no wrong with them. That they will cover up for us in embarrassing moments. That they won't judge us, at least not to our face.

"You can talk about your breasts and how they were hurting the other day when you were having PMS," says twenty-nine-year-old Karalee, Melanie's partner in Diva Productions. "You can talk about your fat thighs and no one's going to judge you for it. I can't go to my guy friends and say, 'Oh man, I'm having the worst cramps.' They can empathize maybe, but they just can't relate."

While her male friendships are equally important to her, Margaret, a twenty-nine-year-old music student, says men are less motivated to put energy into keeping up friendships over time and distance. "I've saved some female friends' positive pep-talk e-mails, and when I get depressed I take them out and read them," she tells me. "My female friendships give me reassurance that I'm a rational human being and a nice person. I get validation."

But male friendships are easier, says twenty-five-year-old Sheela. "You have to work on friendships with women." It's worth it though, she says. "I get so much out of my female friendships. You can't talk to boys about half the stuff you can talk about with girls. You can go from academics to love to drinks in one sentence. I love that!"

"I can't be quite as sloppy around my male friends," says Vicki, a twenty-six-year-old student. "I would never discuss tampons or cramps with them. I'm fortunate to have male friends I love, whom I can have a better time with than with my female friends, but for some reason, I never solve my deep, stupid personal problems with my male friends."

As adult women out in the world away from family, girlfriends become our family, only better because we choose them. "I have one close friend that I have known for about eighteen years," says Fawn, a thirty-year-old in public relations. "It's relationships like that which remind you of who you are and where you have come from and how much you have grown."

For Sarah, a twenty-one-year-old college student, her female friends are like the sisters she never had. And like family, female friendships are always there to come home to even when life sometimes gets in the way.

"It's so important for me to have that ongoing communication," says Miya, a thirty-one-year-old writer. "It can be a month since I've talked to a girlfriend but we just pick up from where we left off. It's like we just talked yesterday."

Girls' Night Out

"'Girls' nights' were unheard of when I was young," says sixty-five-year-old Audrey, the owner of the cabin I rented for a while in order to work on this book. We were sitting in her 150-year-old farmhouse where she had lured me out of my retreat with an invitation to join the family for Thanksgiving dinner. Of course, within five minutes of finishing dinner, the women and men drifted off into separate groups, and I was sitting around talking and laughing with the ladies.

Audrey's comment struck me. I'd never really considered that girls' nights were a new trend—that something I have so come to expect and need hasn't been around forever. Sure, she told me, when she was young, women got together, but there had to be a purpose—quilting or cooking or doing each other's hair. While these get-togethers generated a lot of talk and laughter (what group of women getting together doesn't?), they weren't organized for the sole purpose of going out and having a rip-roaring good time together.

What we did learn from Mom was that whether its quilting or getting dolled up and hitting the clubs together, or staying home ordering pizza, drinking wine, and watching movies together, chillin' with the girls allows us to unwind and let it all hang out. Like bedrooms as teenagers, girls' nights are an essential institution in the Secret Language of Girls.

"You don't have to be on," says Melanie of Diva Productions on the appeal of girls' nights. "You don't have to be sucking your gut in. You don't have to be worrying about that guy around the corner. Not that these are preoccupations, but let's face it, when we're in social situations, we're concerned with how people are viewing us. When you're out with the girls it's one place where you can just be yourself."

"It's that one spot you can go where people aren't really expecting much from you," adds Melanie's partner, Karalee. "If you're a bitch, you can be a bitch. And someone will tell you, 'You're being a bitch.' And you can say, 'Yeah, I know.'"

For Roxanne, girls' nights harken back to the slumber parties of our youth. "They usually involve sitting in someone's bedroom, basement or living room, sometimes drinking together, watching videos or reading magazines," says Roxanne. "My one gay guy friend is the only man ever allowed in, because he's one of the girls. We catch up, discuss school and books, philosophize about life, and plan our futures. Sometimes we sleep over."

Fawn has particular fond memories of a girls' night out that ended up with her and her best girlfriend on all fours at 4 A.M. "I was wearing these enormous six-inch platform boots that I had bought in London, England," she tells me. "These shoes were beautiful but crazy. It was icy and I hit the pavement on a wobbly ankle and ended up smashing my knee and losing a stone out of my favourite ring. My friend Diana went back to the crime scene, scouring the pavement, looking for the missing stone, which she never found. Instead [the next day], she drove to my house with a banged-up glass bead in a beautiful jewel case. It wasn't the stone from the ring, but the thought was so truly lovely."

Margaret likes to go out and eat with her girlfriends, and none of this "Oh, I'll just have a salad—I'm watching my weight" shit, she says. This is also her chance to be "bad." "I have a few friends that I'll smoke with," admits Margaret. "My husband hates it when I smoke, but it feels good to have this secret, off-limits bond with these friends. It's kind of a stupid little act of rebellion."

When you've got the girl posse, it's easier to get a little crazy, take some risks, have the type of adventure you wouldn't have on your own or with a guy. This is especially true when you take girls' night on the road. There is just nothing quite like sailing down the open road with two or three of your best chick friends, windows open, singing "Born to Be Wild" off-key at the top of your fresh-air-filled lungs, looking for adventure in whatever comes your way. Sheer bliss. All-girl road trips are a chance to take your inner bad girl out for a spin. On one of my most memorable road trips, me and a gal pal ended up in a fleabag motel in Whoknowswhere, Kentucky, with a couple of locals. Pure, dirty, fun.

THE RULES (AND NOT THOSE SILLY ONES IN THAT BOOK THAT EVERYONE MADE SUCH A FUSS OVER . . .)

Every girlfriend worth her salt knows the unspoken girlfriend rules. Here are some of the most important ones:

- If she's single and after a guy she knows will be at a certain party/bar/event, we are required to accompany her no matter how tired/stressed/etc. we are.

- Don't flaunt your success in a girlfriend's face. If you're constantly tooting your horn, she won't be really excited for you when something truly incredible happens.

- You must listen to her obsess over every little detail of her new man because you know (at least you hope) one day she will do the same for you.

- You must know when to shut up about your new crush/love interest/lay.

- Don't assume she can always have an hour-long chat every time you call her up. Ask, "Have you got time to talk?" We are there for each other, but we have our own lives.

- No dating one anothers' exes.

- Don't go after a girlfriend's guy—ever.

- Don't go after the same guy/girl. Whoever expresses interest first, gets the first, and only, chance. If she strikes out, the territory is still out of bounds.

- Don't criticize her romantic partner—even if it seems as if they've broken up—until she gives the go-ahead.

- Keep her secrets.

- Assume that anything said to one friend will automatically be repeated to her significant other.

- If a girlfriend is in trouble—depressed, in a bad boyfriend situation, having family problems— she is allowed at least a couple of days of crying and pampering without judgment.

- Never tell the truth if she asks if she looks fat or ugly.

- Stop her from going out looking like a fool, to prevent people from saying, "Doesn't she have any friends to tell her not to wear that?" when they look at her.

- Always believe in each other.

- Never put boys before girls. No man is worth a friendship.

- After a breakup, the guy instantly loses the favour of the girlfriends forever. No matter how wonderful he was, if he doesn't want your friend or if he doesn't work for her, there's got to be something wrong with him because she's the greatest girl who ever lived.

- Stand behind each other's decisions.

- Know when to say something about her decisions like, "Whoa, are you sure you're doing the right thing?" or "That doesn't suit you at all," but always be sure to add, "If you really want to do it, I'll still love you."

- If someone is putting your friend down, stick up for her.

- Call back right away.

- Rat on her boyfriend if you see something inappropriate.

- Never work for a close girlfriend or hire a close girlfriend to work under you.

- If you've been friends for a long time and have never lived together, don't move in together; it usually wrecks the friendship.

- Never befriend a known enemy.

- *Always* remember birthdays.

"Road tripping is an autoerotic adventure where you get to do the things you don't allow yourself to do at home," says Cameron Tuttle, author of *The Bad Girl's Guide to the Open Road*. Eat like a pig. Wear the same underwear for days. Go-go dance in a wet tube top. Flirt with strangers." But you have to mind your road trip manners, says Tuttle. "If you're a true road sister, common courtesy requires that the cute chick doesn't always get the guy," she explains. "In fact, it's her duty to do whatever she can to help the other girls get laid." Even if that means three of you have to pretend to be lesbians, as Tuttle once did, so a fourth could get some action. "I wouldn't have the guts to do that at home," she admits. That's why road trips are so much fun. You get to be and do whatever the hell you want. With no witnesses.

We Need to Talk

And yes, most importantly, we get to talk to each other. By now, the Secret Language we share is fully formed and essential to our relationships with other women. In his long-running Broadway solo show, *Defending the Caveman*, Rob Becker explains women's incessant need to talk. "So, here's how it works," he says. "Men were the hunters, see? They were required to stand side by side without talking for fear they'd scare off the prey." Women, on the other hand, as gatherers out foraging in the jungle for food, had to talk for their own safety. "If a woman goes for too long without hearing the voice of another woman, she knows she's been eaten by an animal," Becker jokes. As a result, women are genetically allotted some five thousand words a day, while men are allotted only two thousand. No wonder women talk more, Becker concludes. Actually, I believe it's seven thousand for women, but who's arguing?

"We always have something else to say," admits Tamara, a twenty-eight-year-old marketing manager. "If we didn't have to work or sleep, it would never end." Among all the women I talked to, as much fun as they had messing with boys' heads in bars or watching bad movies together, every single woman said the number-one thing they like to do when they get together with girlfriends is talk. Sit and talk, listen to music and talk, stay up all night and talk, laugh and talk and drink wine and talk, eat and talk. . . . And when I asked what they liked to talk about, most of them said the better question would be, "What don't we talk about?" "We can spend all evening talking about everything from world issues, religion, hopes, fears, and career aspirations to the latest skirt length," says Fawn. "That's what is so great about women."

Just as you needed to tell your girlfriends everything you were going through as a teenager, as adults we need to share our experiences with other women. "Whether it's discussions about relationships, or crazy bosses, or what I should wear to a particular event, my girlfriends always help me with whatever I'm dealing with," says Amy, a twenty-five-year-old research assistant. "That's not to say that at times you don't find your friends (or people you thought were your friends) infuriating, or that 'breaking up' with them isn't possible. In fact, it's far more difficult than any boy breakup I've ever had."

According to anthropologist and *The First Sex* author Helen Fisher, study after study in practically every culture of the world has found that women talk more than men do. "They've also found that women's basic articulation skills and her ability to find the right word rapidly goes up in the middle of the menstrual cycle when estrogen levels peak," says Fisher. Women are built to use words to communicate, to acquire support, to educate, and to connect.

"I Love Your Boots!"

And it's not just what we say but how we say it. Studies have shown that women use more emotional language than men who use more direct, goal-oriented language. According to Claire A. Etaugh and Judith S. Bridges, authors of *The Psychology of Women: A Lifespan Perspective*, women are more likely than men to use intrusive adverbs—for example, "She is really friendly"—whereas men tend to use directives—"Think about this."

Women also use verbs that express uncertainty—"It seems that the class will be very interesting."—or hedging—

"I kind of feel you should not be too upset about this."
Women tend to check in with whomever they're talking to
by asking questions like "Do you agree?"

One might conclude from this seemingly tentative conversation style that women are less confident when they speak,
worrying about what they say and how it will be received.
This might seem true when you compare it with the way
men talk. They might see our uncertainty as unauthoritative.
But that's not the case. Women regard this as a way of including other women, keeping the lines of communication open,
and inviting others to share their opinions. We learn to read
between each other's lines.

And to read each other's body language. Women, say
Etaugh and Bridges, are more likely than men to engage in
non-verbal behaviours, like smiling, for example, that demon-
strate interpersonal interest and warmth. As a result, women
have developed an entire Secret Language that goes way
beyond the words being spoken; it's a combination of words,
intonations, subtle eyebrow lifts, and well-placed pauses that
men simply do not understand. "Women tend to talk in half
sentences and almost thought pictures," says Kimberly. "We
can say something to one another, and know what the other
means, even though half of what was meant was left unsaid."

Margaret tells me about being in a room with a group
of people listening to some boring guy blab on and on. "I
thought I was going to die," she recalls. "Then I looked over
at the woman next to me and caught her eye. Within seconds,

a non-verbal message flashed between us: This man is stupid. I am so bored."

The great thing about this kind of non-verbal communication is that it crosses language barriers. A good friend of mine was in Cuba recently and this guy was hitting on her while a Cuban woman looked on. My friend said she rolled her eyes at the woman, who smiled back knowingly. They didn't speak the same language, but in one shared look they were able to communicate so much about the universal experience of women.

Of course, non-verbal communication between women isn't always so sisterly. "I hate that weird competitive vibe I sometimes get," says Margaret. "With some women, I feel like they automatically size me up as competition for men. If I'm with my husband or a male friend and I encounter one of these women, they act as though I'm not there and spend the entire time talking to the guy I'm with." Which is why I always go out of my way to compliment a woman when her boyfriend or husband introduces us. "I love your boots! Where did you get them?" becomes a way of saying, I'm on your side, and I'm not a threat. We can be friends.

Sociolinguist Janet Holmes of Victoria University in Wellington, New Zealand, writes about how women use compliments to establish connections in *Language and Gender: A Reader*. Holmes studied the distribution of compliments between New Zealand women and men and found that women gave 68 per cent of all compliments recorded.

By contrast, only 9 per cent of the men complimented each other. Women, Holmes found, appeared to use compliments as a way to be polite and create rapport, in order to establish and maintain relationships.

Women also tend to be more physical in their communication. We tend to touch each other on the arm, hand, or shoulder more often in conversation to make a point or to let the other person know we empathize. Part of this is no doubt due to the fact that as schoolgirls and teenagers, it was more acceptable for us to be physically intimate with each other. "I'm perfectly comfortable hugging people hello and goodbye, while my husband is more restrained," says Margaret. "I think it's easier and more acceptable for women to show strong emotions like happiness and sadness openly."

Brothers from Another Planet

There has been plenty written about men and women's differing communication styles. Deborah Tannen's 1991 classic, *You Just Don't Understand: Men and Women in Conversation* is often cited for its analysis of how men engage in "report" talk and women in "rapport" talk.

Jennifer Coates, a professor of English language and linguistics in England and author of *Women, Men and Language: A Sociolinguistic Account of Gender Differences in Language* has also studied communication patterns in women-only and men-only groups and come up with similar results. Coates says that women reveal a lot about their private lives in order to establish and maintain connection in conversation. They also stick to one topic for a long time, let all speakers finish their sentences and try to let everyone participate.

Men, on the other hand, rarely talk about their personal relationships and feelings but "compete to prove themselves better informed about current affairs, travel, sport, etc." The topics change often, and men try to "establish a reasonably stable hierarchy, with some men dominating conversation and others talking very little."

Women will also keep the thread of a conversation going by picking up on what their friends have said and linking it to a similar topic of her own, says Coates. Men tend to ignore what has been said before and concentrate on making their own point, even if it has nothing to do with what was said before.

Next time you're in a café, watch a pair of women talking. You'll notice a lot of nodding. Listen to one side of a phone conversation between two women and you'll hear "Uh-huh," "Really?" and "Yeah, I know what you mean." Women use these types of interruptions as a way of showing that they are actively listening and supporting the person they are speaking with. Men don't do this, and women often accuse them of not listening. Men interrupt only if they intend to take the floor, says Coates, which implies that the current speaker cannot finish her/his turn. "As a consequence, in mixed-sex conversations, women often feel they are not being respected, so they will speak less than men and are hurt as such behaviour violates the rules of their co-operatively organized conversational style."

We also ask more questions, don't we? Women use questions as another way to show we're listening, according to authors Etaugh and Bridge in *The Psychology of Women*. Of course, we're less interested in the answers than in keeping the conversation flowing. Men, however, see questions as a request for information, say Etaugh and Bridge because for men communication is more about impressing others with how much they know, so they are happy to launch into a detailed answer.

I notice with my women friends that we take turns holding the floor. I know that if I let my friend unload, she's eventually gonna turn and ask me what's going on with me and then it's my turn to vent. If that doesn't happen, it bugs me. Guys don't usually work like that. Ever been on a date with a guy and he's doing all the talking while you're doing all the listening wondering if he's ever going to ask you anything about yourself? I thought so.

"No matter how hard I try and despite twenty years of working in an industry that's dominated by men, I still tend to talk differently to men," says Kathy, who works in communications technology and, at forty-one, is married with four sons. "I have this feeling that I have to dazzle them with my brilliance and my wide range of knowledge so I choose every word carefully and I seldom offer an opinion that I can't back up. With women I never feel the need to impress —we just sit back and 'spill.'"

Women often complain that men try to solve our problems. What they fail to realize is that when we are whining about our friendships or problems at work, we're usually not looking for a solution—we're looking for someone to empathize and say "Poor you" or "That must be awful for you." When he gives us his opinion or tells us what he thinks we should do, we think, Didn't he hear me? and get angry.

"Women tend to show understanding of another woman's feelings," say Etaugh and Bridge. "When men try to reassure women by telling them that their situation is not so bleak, the women hear their feelings being belittled or discounted." We need him to understand that, on some level, we know it's not that bleak, but right now it feels bleak, and goddammit, we want him to acknowledge this.

"Most of the time a woman would prefer that you tell her you've heard how she feels and understand that she feels that way rather than try to offer solutions for situations that upset her," says Dana, a thirty-six-year-old Web developer. "It's more important to be heard and rescue yourself than to have someone try to rescue you."

That's not to say the women necessarily talk more than men, despite the fact that historically women have been ridiculed and punished for talking too much. In study after study today, it's men who talk more in meetings, in mixed sex classrooms, and on dates. In other words, men feel comfortable speaking in public while women feel more comfortable speaking in private. That's why when a guy gets home at the end of the day, his girlfriend or wife wants to talk. She's been out in the world being quiet all day and he's been out talking. For men, the privacy of home becomes a place where they don't have to talk any more, where they are free from having to prove themselves and impress people with their knowledge. But for women, home is a place where they are free to talk, where they feel the greatest need for talk. For them, the comfort of home means the freedom to talk without worrying about how their talk will be judged.

"With men I tend to talk about what's happening on a specific day, about people we know in common, or about work, school, or life in general. I tend to avoid really personal topics because they always seem so mystified and either fascinated or turned off by the stuff I talk about with women," says twenty-seven-year-old Tracy.

The truth is, we don't really want guys to communicate the same way as our girlfriends, do we? Ever see that episode of *Friends* in which Rachel is dating Ross's young girlfriend's dad (played by Bruce Willis)? She pushes him to open up and then is completely turned off by his emotional outpouring. We want our guys to be vulnerable, but not too much. That's scary. Our girlfriends, on the other hand, can be as vulnerable as they want, and it makes us closer. But even girlfriends can get too needy. I've had to break up with friends because I started to feel as if we were in more of a relationship than a friendship.

Not all women seek out this kind of emotional connection through verbal communication. Some even avoid it.

WAIT TILL YOU HEAR THIS!

Men have always detested women's gossip because they suspect the truth: their measurements are being taken and compared. – Erica Jong

There is nothing quite so seductive as having a friend call you up or whisper with anticipation the moment they see you, "Have I got something to tell you."

I admit it. I love to gossip. Who doesn't? Oh, c'mon. You're gonna tell me you've never sat with a friend and talked about another friend or enjoyed the sinful delight of trashing another woman's outfit or giving each other a play-by-play about the horrible thing that guy in the corner supposedly did to a friend of a friend.

Sure, women can talk about everything, but it's the secrecy surrounding gossip that makes it so special. And the fact that you're not gonna share this dirt with just anyone. The recipient has to be special. When a friend has good gossip for us, we feel privileged to be the recipient. And because we are part of the inside group—that is, the ones gossiping rather than being gossiped about—we feel connected.

Exchanging dirt is also the quickest way to bond. It's also just plain fun. "As sick as this is, sometimes it can be fun to rip someone apart for the sole purpose of easing your own insecurities," admits Tiffany, an eighteen-year-old student. "I do indulge in it, even though I think it's wrong."

The origin of the word "gossip" has been traced back to the fourteenth century, when the godparent of a child was referred to as "God-sibb" or "God-sibling." It went on to apply to someone belonging to the group from which godparents would typically be chosen. At the time, the birth of a child was one of the few acceptable occasions for women to come together. The term "gosibb" and eventually gossip, expanded to describe this activity. Gathered together around the new mother, they no doubt gossiped about events and people of their community. By 1811, The *Oxford English Dictionary* described gossip as "idle talk, trifling or groundless rumour; tittle-tattle" and a gossip was described as "one who runs about tattling like women at a lying-in."

This new meaning trivialized female communication. Part of this came out of fear, as I mentioned in an earlier chapter, of the subversive nature of gossip. As long as we didn't let women get together and talk, about what jerks men were, for example, they would stay put in the kitchen and the bedroom. Soon, our sexual reputation became tied into how much we gossiped. Gossip was described as "loose talk" and women who engaged in it were "busybodies."

After spending time with northern Canadian women, Mary Crnkovich found that written histories of the

North tend to ignore women's experiences because these women rely so heavily on oral tradition. According to Crnkovich (in a 1989 publication she edited titled *Gossip: A Spoken History of Women in the North*), "the word 'gossip,' when used pejoratively to describe communication between women has tended to isolate them from one another by trivializing their everyday experiences. It is in this way that their accounts and perspectives have been neglected or marginalized in written records." Thanks to all this, we now feel tremendously guilty when we gossip. Most women I talked to either flat-out refuse to admit that they participate in gossip, or they admit to it apologetically or with qualifiers. "My girlfriends and I usually will justify it as 'not gossiping, but discussing our concern for so and so,'" says Roxanne. "My friends and I are not trash talkers for the sake of trash talking." Breanna, a seventeen-year-old secretary, described gossip as "a very powerful evil that just won't stop controlling me."

There's no denying that malicious gossip can be evil and downright nasty and that women use it against other women. But Roxanne admits that there is a good side to gossiping. "It helps me organize my world and understand what is going on with other friends." Sometimes we need to "consult" one friend about another friend about a situation or a problem we can't resolve with her directly, either because we've tried and hit a brick wall or because we think it would hurt her feelings or start a fight to be honest with her.

Melanie Telbutt outlines the positive aspects of gossip in her book *Women's Talk?* She believes that talk of friends, relatives, and acquaintances shapes our social values. "An analysis of the gossip of a specific time and place can tell us much more about the rules governing a particular group's behaviour," writes Telbutt. "One of the many purposes of gossip in our ancestors was that it was a vital form of spreading the news. Gossip was the daily newspaper," says anthropologist Helen Fisher.

When someone says, "Any new gossip?" what they mean is, "What's new?" Gossiping keeps us in the loop. It also bonds us. "Back when I was a waitress, I found no faster way to establish friendships with the other waitresses than to gossip about people at various tables," admits thirty-year-old Susan, an administrative assistant. "Even now, in my office, I feel an instant bond with another female if we both agree over some catty remark."

Karen, thirty-seven, says she actually finds it easier to communicate with men because they don't expect the same kind of emotional intimacy as her female friends. Twenty-eight-year-old Lesa, an assistant editor at a fashion magazine, says the thing she likes least about her communication with women is, as she gently puts it, "the overly sensitive, emotional bullshit."

I've also met men who never shut up and overanalyze interpersonal relationships even more than I do. Suzette Elgin, author of *Genderspeak*, thinks that our differing communication styles have more to do with power than gender. When you switch the power, you switch the language behaviour, she says. For example, when a female trial lawyer cross-examines a male witness, the lawyer will use a direct style of communication associated with men. Since men are statistically more often in power positions, we associate the dominant style of communication with men.

What Should I Do?

There's no denying that women spend an inordinate amount of time talking about and analyzing relationships. Hey, how else are we supposed to learn from other people's mistakes? As I've often said, when women need sex or relationship advice, we don't call a therapist or an expert or a male friend —we go to our girlfriends.

"Men, even gay men, can never be as empathetic as women when it comes to this stuff," says Alexia, a twenty-two-year-old waitress and massage therapy student from Quebec. "When it comes to relationship problems, I will call my girlfriends first, get everything off my chest, and then talk to boyfriends about problems once they have been sorted out."

The tradition of women giving each other relationship advice no doubt goes back to the dawn of time, but the first public example can be traced back to the 1890s, with one of the first agony aunts, Annie Swan, and her column in the magazine *Women at Home*.

Annie Swan (a pseudonym) was a well-known author at the time according to Margaret Beetham's book, *Magazine of her Own?: Domesticity and Desire in the Woman's Magazine, 1800–1914*, and "a female figure who was mature but not 'old,' who treated her correspondents' problems with the attention due to equals. In her 'Over the Teacups' column, she encouraged readers to write in, using the confessional mode to discuss their personal relationships, especially the romantic and marital," says Beetham, a professor of Victorian and women's writing at Manchester Metropolitan University in England. Unlike previous advice columns by men that employed "a jovial masculine authority, Swan offered sympathy and moral seriousness in a thoroughly feminine persona." "Over the Teacups," became a place where women could exchange confidences and be equals as friends. The illustration for the column showed a group of seated women facing one another with no obvious authority figure. In the same way, my girlfriends and I sit around a kitchen or restaurant table dissecting one another's lives and offering advice.

"Giving relationship advice is part of the girlfriend code," says Rachel, a twenty-three-year-old special projects coordinator at a non-profit organization. "We all need to learn from each other, because girlfriends can see things about you that you may not be ready to admit." That doesn't mean we need our girlfriends telling us what to do. In fact, advice is probably the wrong word for it. While we are happy to talk about relationships, what's wrong with men, and our own personal struggles with love, when we turn to a friend in a moment of relationship crisis, the last thing we want them to do is tell us what they really think.

"I would rather drink my own day-old urine than give any of my girlfriends relationship advice," Margaret bluntly puts it. "Chances are good that if I were to give advice, they would turn around and do something completely different and then resent me for even suggesting that there might be a better way to go about things." Again, our friends are usually just looking for a place to vent or to have their views reinforced or to reassure themselves that after weighing options, they are doing the right thing. If we do give advice, we make sure it's something she's going to be comfortable with.

"Once a girlfriend got really mad at me because I told her that the guy she was dating was too old for her," recalls Devalina, a twenty-two-year-old student. "She got mad because she said she never told me what she thought was wrong with the guys I went out with. They ended up having a bad breakup, and we worked it out. I never said 'I told you so.'"

And it works both ways. "When and if a friend of mine tries to give me advice (in other words, tries to tell me what she thinks I should do)," says Margaret, "I thank her for her concern and then do whatever the hell I want to do. I try to remember that said friend isn't trying to find fault with my own judgment; she's just trying to be helpful and this is the way she thinks she can help. I don't think I would be close friends with someone who was constantly expressing disapproval of my judgment. I have faith that my friends are smart and will eventually find, perhaps through trial and error, what is right for them."

That doesn't mean we don't tuck their comments away for a rainy day. Dana says she usually does what she wants when her friends give her advice but admits the advice can influence her choices. "Even when I don't take their advice, I store it away in case it turns out I should have listened to them."

The twisted part of the deal is that even if we don't take our friend's advice, we still expect them to back us up no matter what we do. To a point, anyway. "I let my girlfriends know that I don't want to hear the same old shit all the time if they're not willing to get off their asses and help themselves out of their situations," says Roxanne. Not that we'd put it quite so bluntly.

Kate Fillion writes in her 1996 book *Lip Service: The Truth about Women's Darker Side in Love, Sex and Friendship* that much of our bonding with other women is based on ripping men apart. "Women's sharing and caring frequently involves swapping stories about what jerks men are and diminishing men to shore each other up," writes Fillion. "Making fun of men is a quick and easy way to establish common ground and bond with other women. *They're all just little boys masquerading in suits. They're scared of strong, intelligent women.*

They'll do anything to get sex. They don't care about anyone except themselves." In other words, says Fillion, women's connection is not just based on our great ability to empathize with each other but on having a common adversary—men.

Talking Dirty

Probably the only thing women love talking about more than men and relationships is sex. The two often overlap, but while relationship talk is often full of angst and pondering, talking about sex is often pure pleasure. I've barely got my pants on after I've slept with some new guy and I'm on the blower to the girls.

"Hi, howzit going, howz work? I finally slept with Richard."

"What! Oh my God. How was it!?"

"He was very sweet. Shy, but sweet. And very, um, attentive."

"Oral?"

"Yes, excellent. Great tongue."

"Did you have intercourse?"

"Yeah, sort of.

"What do you mean, sort of?"

"Well, he kinda lost his erection when we put the condom on."

"Oh no, not one of those. Think it's chronic?"

"No, I think he was just nervous. He was cool about it.
We just did other stuff."

"Size?"

"Pretty good. Been with bigger, been with smaller.'

"Gonna see him again?"

"I hope so; we had a good time. Dinner was nice.
We clicked."

Maybe we're making up for lost time. As little girls, we were encouraged to suppress our sexuality, whereas masturbation is practically a rite of passage for boys. Everyone expects them to do it. You never see coy references in the movies to what that little girl might be doing with her Wrinkles dog or how we first discovered the joys of water jets. Between the code of silence around our early sexuality and the years of messages that we must control our sexuality, it's as if our inner slut comes out and we suddenly can't shut up about it. Besides, there's too much valuable information to share. Was your first time as bad as mine was? When did you have your first orgasm? What's your favourite toy and where do I get one?

Whether it's for advice, tips, or just for the sheer pleasure of living vicariously through a friend's particularly raucous sexual experience, talking to your girlfriends about your sex life can be tremendously useful. It's a chance to gush, especially early in a relationship when you're not ready to let him know the extent of your feelings. A girlfriend can also put things into perspective and remind you of your short-term memory: "You said the exact same thing about Peter," when you proclaim, "I reeeally feel like this one is different!"

Later on in the relationship, talking to a girlfriend about your sex life is good for test-driving a discussion topic before you bring it up with him. By bouncing your thoughts off a friend, you sort out your feelings, figure out if there are solutions you could exercise on your own, and come up with the best way to raise the issue with him. If there are sexual problems, your girlfriend may have had a similar experience and can help normalize the situation so you don't get too freaked out by it. Very reassuring.

Often, we don't even have to go into graphic detail. Experiences are common enough that after a few well-placed eyebrow raises, a few nods, and a couple of heavy sighs, our friend is onboard. "Oh, right, I've been with guys who can't get it up too," we commiserate. "Listen, here's what I did."

That's not to say that there is no such a thing as too much information. I don't really need to picture my girlfriend's boyfriend handcuffed, tied from the ceiling, clad in her favourite bra and panties. It might make me a little uncomfy next time we all go out to the movies together. You have to know where to draw the line.

Of course, sometimes you just gotta tell it like it is. And then, yes, we get very graphic. Guys always seem surprised at how graphic we get. "We always talk about sex," says nineteen-year-old Paula, a university student. "It's our favourite topic. We go into a lot of detail sometimes (usually when there are drinks around), like how good it was, the size, how long it lasted, how many times we did it, his expressions, noises, funny things that happen, stuff like that." In many ways, it seems like a perfectly natural extension of women's already intimate verbal interactions.

Melody recounts how she recently found herself in the waiting room of a clinic engaged in an intense discussion about G-spots with a bunch of women she'd never met. Apparently, someone had read something in *Cosmo* that launched the discussion.

It's more fun to be crass with women, says Rachel. "Men tend to be put off by women discussing sex, particularly the failings of some men," she says. "With women, you can let it all hang out. With men, you run the risk of freaking them out and making them uncomfortable."

"We go into intense, gross detail, like the look and feel of an individual dick, specific methods of coming, present or absent juices, colours, textures, time periods, locations, positions—nothing is left untalked about," says Roxanne. Tiffany says the last conversation she had with her girlfriends was about anal sex and "rainbow kisses" or "red angels"—both terms that refer to going down on a woman when she has her period.

Carlyle Jansen runs Good for Her, a sex toy shop in Toronto geared to women. She too admits to being very graphic with her girlfriends when it comes to sex. "We share experiences and bloopers—what worked and what didn't," says Jansen. "I talk about it the way I would if I went on a hike and explored mud pools and forests and animal tracks.

I get validation for what I might think is weird. I show off what I have learned." Besides the graphic detail, Jansen also believes that unlike most men, women also talk about sex more in context of a relationship. For example, she says, "A woman will say, 'We had sex under the stars and I felt so close to him/her' or 'We fucked in the alley and s/he is so hot. I couldn't believe we did it' or 'We have great sex. Things are really good.'"

"Women are more open and less concerned about how we come off to our friends," says Sapna, a twenty-seven-year-old publicist. "It's less about bragging and more about bonding and sharing. We're not socialized to always perform and excel. I think a lot of men get into the macho thing and have a hard time expressing insecurities."

"It's almost like men talking about cars," says Sarah."It's something we care about fixing and making the best we can, and we want to use the correct terminology so that we all know what we're talking about. On the rare occasion that I've talked to a guy like that, he just looked at me like 'I can't believe you just said that.' I'm just more honest with my girlfriends."

The Other "C" Word

We may be honest with each other about our oral sex habits during menstruation, but that doesn't mean women can be honest with each other about everything. Like feelings of competition, for example. Even today, if a man is called competitive, he's usually being praised; if a woman is called competitive, she's a bitch or a ball breaker.

Men seem to enjoy a little healthy conflict, even among friends. "My father-in-law enjoys arguing just for the sport of it—I hate this. I think most women see argument as a means to an end and not an activity unto itself," says Margaret. "As a woman, I don't understand why you would argue with another person over a subject you have little personal investment in."

Women greet each other with compliments—"You look great!" "I love your outfit!"—and questions—"How are you doing?" (and we actually want to know). We'll even put ourselves down to avoid competition. After our friends tell us we look great, we say, "I feel like shit." When she says she likes our hair, we tell her hers looks better. We do everything to avoid making anyone feel superior or better. In other words, we do everything to smooth over any competitive feelings. Helen Fisher believes part of this is biological. "Women learned to develop support systems [because] rearing our young takes many, many years, and requires a stable network for a long period of time," she tells me. "It's adaptive to build that network and to remember when you've been betrayed."

Just like the young girls I spoke with, most adult women also said that betraying trust is one of the worse things a girlfriend can do. As women, we have a lot invested in getting along. The idea that men are competitive and that is bad and women are co-operative and this is good is a holdover from the seventies when feminists declared the sisterhood. Competition feels like a betrayal of the sisterhood. "Competition is considered unfeminine. It's, well, not nice," writes Leora Tanenbaum in *Slut!*. "Girls and women are socialized to be polite, to say 'Please' and 'Thank you' and 'You're welcome,'" says Tanenbaum. "This tension between covert competition and the social pressure to be nice to other women and girls pushes the competitive spirit into the surreptitious realm of gossip, backstabbing and undermining."

The way we express competition, then, becomes part of the Secret Language. As Fisher puts it, "a man will punch you in the face, and women will stab you in the back. Women are more likely to do it with words, men with fists."

"When women feel safe with each other, we're much more likely to voice inner fears, questions, and feelings that we wouldn't voice to anyone else," says Kate, a twenty-six-year-old student and Web designer. "When women feel insecure around each other, that's when it can get hurtful, bitchy, and cold." Part of this is because we have so much invested in our interpersonal relationships. We take things more personally. "Women get offended more easily," says Aimée, a twenty-two-year-old midwifery student. "They'll accept an apology before they're ready and then nurse silent, deep grudges."

Hard Feelings

The truth is, we don't know what to do with feelings of competition with other women. While we often have no trouble criticizing or expressing anger and hurt to our boyfriend or husband, we have a harder time getting angry with a girlfriend.

Louise Eichenbaum and Susie Orbach, the authors of *Between Women: Love, Envy, and Competition in Women's Friendships*, believe part of this goes back to our relationship with our mothers, to something they called "merged attachment." By this they refer to the difficulty we have seeing where our mother ends and we begin. This merged attachment is often carried into our female friendships. "Women's psychology is currently constructed in such a way that her capacities to be close and giving and her fear of separation are psychologically inseparable." When a friendship shifts, it stirs up some of the same emotions we felt trying to separate ourselves from outgrowing our mothers.

Female friends prefer to remain equal. They are different personality-wise, sure, but equal in the world. We need this in order to be able to commiserate about our lot in life, the things that hold us back, and our universal experiences. Just like back in high school, we want to fit in. Being different means not fitting in and that's scary. It makes us feel as if we'll be abandoned and alone.

So instead of telling our friend what we really think about her situation, we support her take on it, even alter our own experiences to fit into her world view in order to make her feel loved and have her love us back. All this goes against competition, which is all about differentiating yourself, about breaking ranks.

When a female friend does well, for example, as much as we are happy for her, part of us gets a little freaked. We may not be as supportive as we could be; we may even try and hold her back in subtle ways, by perhaps making her question herself or belittling some aspect of her achievement. This is not about wanting to be mean but rather about our fear of being left in our friend's dust. Or about wanting what she has.

Women tend to feel envious rather than competitive. It is far easier for most women to admit that we envy another woman than to recognize that we are competing with her because competition means difference and separation. So instead we envy whatever other women have—be it material, physical, or intellectual—that disconnects her from us. "Some women attract other women's envy the way honey attracts bears," writes Laura Tracy in *The Secret between Us: Competition among Women*. "They have only to walk into a room to make all the other women there miserable—hating themselves, loathing her."

When we deny our own competitiveness with each other we feel bonded and intimate, but we also deny the reality of our individual lives. "Some women want power; some don't," says Tracey. "Some want children, or men; some don't.

When we assume that bonding with each other depends on denying individual desires, we impose our own versions of reality on each other, and by doing so, we lose choice."

Don't Hate Me Because I'm Beautiful

At the same time that women are discouraged from being outwardly competitive, we live in a culture that constantly sets women up to compete, especially when it comes to our appearance and to men.

An ad in *Chatelaine* magazine in the 1950s describes "a girdle that makes your figure so beautiful, other women will hate you." And remember that shampoo ad from the eighties with the slogan "Don't Hate Me Because I'm Beautiful?"

Competition among women has historically centred on competing with each other for men's attention through our appearance. At the same time, from adolescence on, women talk about going after the same guy as one of the most unforgivable things another woman can do. The conflict can really mess you up, as Tanya, a twenty-five-year-old mental health housing worker, knows. She is constantly struggling with competing with other women for men's attention. She believes that men are primarily interested in women's chests and waists sizes and doesn't feel she measures up. As a result, she compares herself with other women and is obsessed with what she eats and how much physical exercise she gets. But Tanya doesn't let other women know how strongly competitive she feels next to them; it's a secret preoccupation.

We all do it. We do it so much that after a while it becomes difficult to know if we're trying to look good for men or, as so many women have argued and men have suspected, simply for each other. Just as we measured ourselves against the other girls—who got the first bra or who got her period first—as adults we measure our looks and our lives against other women's. Except we don't see it as trying to compete but as trying to fit in. Just as in high school, if we have the right clothes, we won't be left out of the clique.

We're All in This Together

Rather than compete, we commiserate. We bond over the very thing we are expected to compete over. In her book of the same name, Naomi Wolf talks about how "The Beauty Myth" creates camaraderie between women. "A wry smile about calories, a complaint about one's hair can evaporate the sullen examination of a rival in the fluorescent light of a ladies' room," says Wolf.

Anthropologists Mimi Nichter and Nancy Vuckovic have found that "fat talk"—repeatedly using expressions like "I'm so fat"—is a way of being part of a group, since it requires the listeners to jump in and say, "No you're not." It's a way of saying, Hey girls, we may feel competitive, but it's not our fault. We are all victims of the same cultural pressures and messages that we are not allowed to be feminine and ambitious, that we must compete with each other for male attention. It's not our fault that we constantly have to prove ourselves. It's as if we're all in on one big conspiracy that's beyond our control and this helps smooth away feelings of competitiveness about our looks, our attractiveness, our worth.

Looking Good, Girl!

I'm tired of all this nonsense about beauty being only skin-deep. That's deep enough. What do you want— an adorable pancreas?

— JEAN KERR, American author and playwright

Looking good isn't all about competing to attract men. The beauty rituals we learn as woman are a huge part of the Secret Language. They bond us as women. Finding the perfect shade of lipstick or spending an afternoon at the spa getting primped and plucked doesn't necessarily mean we are help-less victims buying into a culture that judges us on our appear-ance. Some of us, gulp, actually enjoy this stuff. It's part of being a girl and something we learn from a young age.

"I learned about makeup by watching my sister Darlene and my mother—she always did her face really nicely," recalls sixty-year-old Lorraine. "I'd go into Mom's bedroom and muck around with her things. In our house, there'd often be two of us in the bathroom—one going pee while the other was having a bath—so we just learned about stuff like shaving our legs from observing one another."

Mom may have made a big deal about our period being our ticket to womanhood, but for me that moment came about a year later, the first time I put makeup on in front of my sister's Kenmore mirror—the one with the day, night, and office settings. Somehow, sweeping on that peacock blue eyeshadow, brushing those two streaks of cheap chalky blush over my cheeks and slicking on my coral lipstick made me feel a lot more womanly than pinning a three-inch thick pad to my undies.

Putting Our Best Face Forward

Twenty-eight year-old Renee has been a makeup artist for MAC cosmetics for six years. She's been into makeup since she was five and started sneaking her mother's lipstick. "I'd come out with bright red lips and try to tell my mom I didn't have any lipstick on," she says, laughing. "I think that we want to ape our mothers," says Renee by way of explaining makeup's appeal to women. "We want approval from our elders, so we want to look mature and be taken more seriously. And I did feel pretty."

While it may seem women are genetically born with the ability to draw a straight line on a curved eyelid or to know how to operate eyelash curlers, ironically many of us learned our best tricks from Mom. Sara, a twenty-four-year-old communications assistant, remembers sitting at her mother's vanity table and being shown how to apply eyeshadow and to use cold cream to take it off at night. "My mom was the person who got me hooked on this whole painting-your-face thing, and it stuck," says Sara.

Krista's grandmother used to let her do makeovers on her, and her mother let her play with her makeup. "From watching my mom, I learned that mascara is very, very important. Even if my mother wears no other makeup, she almost always puts on mascara."

Twenty-one-year-old Jesse's mom taught her that no matter how much makeup you put on, she should always make it look subtle. Her mom also took her to have her colours done when she was young. "I was classified as a winter, which meant using certain shades like blues and bright pinks as opposed to olive greens and mauves."

Paula's mom always put on her "face" whenever she went out—whether it was to go grocery shopping or to a dinner party. As a result, even though Paula doesn't like wearing makeup, she feels too self-conscious not to wear it. "I like it because it covers all my flaws and imperfections, and I feel 'pretty' with it on," she says.

"Sometimes I feel bad when I don't have makeup on because I just don't feel like I look as good as I can," says thirty-one-year-old Carla, a fitness instructor. "Like my mother always says, 'You never know who you're gonna meet in a day,' so I feel like I should look my best most of the time. I might meet my Prince Charming!" And apparently he'll like you better with a bunch of crap on your face.

Truth be told, most straight men will say they just don't get the whole makeup thing. Or that they prefer us *au naturel*. Of course, they're the first to ask if you're feeling okay when you're not wearing any makeup. But beyond that, most guys just don't get it. For women, makeup is about much more than just looking pretty.

"The search for the right lipstick is a never-ending quest," writes Véronique Vienne in *Read My Lips: A Cultural History of Lipstick*. "If I could invent the ultimate color it would be called 'Perfect Shade,'" says *Harper's Bazaar* editor Annmarie Iverson in *Read My Lips*. "It would be that perfect plummy, pinky, browny, neutral that, when I put it on, makes me look younger, thinner, taller, smarter, healthier. That's the dream of lipstick. If you choose the right color, it can do everything." The 92 per cent of women who wear lipstick know its transformative powers. As Diana Ross said, "Without lipstick I look tired." Even if you wear no other makeup, a swipe of lipstick after dinner or before you head into a meeting gives you that extra boost of confidence. Some women who wear makeup are so accustomed to it that they don't consider themselves makeup users. "I don't wear much makeup at all, especially because I go to the gym a lot and it would just get wrecked," says Leah, a twenty-nine-year-old freelance writer. "But I will never go out without concealer, mascara, and lipstick. This one friend says, 'You're wearing makeup,' but that's totally not makeup to me; that's my face."

"I justify it this way," jokes Brigitte Gall, host of the television show *World's Greatest Spas*, "I have blond hair. Basically, without some eyebrow pencil and some mascara, my head just looks like a white orb on my very large shoulders."

Can I Borrow Your Lipstick?

While I love makeup and take great pleasure in trying new techniques and new colours, I have to admit I do occasionally look at my twenty tubes of barely used lipstick and think, Wait a minute. What have I bought into here? It's not just the implication that we're not good enough as we are, but it's also the promise that we can be even better with yet another brand-new shade of lipstick.

"I love mascara and lip gloss, but I get embarrassed by the attention I get wearing much more makeup than that," says Roxanne. "It's good attention, but I always get a little depressed, thinking, What? I'm not noticeably pretty all the time? Sometimes I don't like being rewarded for fitting the girl standard."

Kathy Peiss addresses this conflict in her book, *Hope in a Jar: The Making of America's Beauty Culture*. "What do women declare when they 'put on a face'?" she writes. "It may seem that the promise of beauty is nothing but a commercial myth that binds women to its costly pursuit. Critics are not wrong to address the power of corporations, advertisement, and mass media to foster and profit from this myth. But they have overlooked the web of intimate rituals, social relationships, and female institutions that gave form to American beauty culture." Before the cosmetics industry took hold, says Mcgowan, many women concocted their own cosmetics, using natural oils and herbs brought to America by its different immigrant communities.

Englishwomen of the seventeenth and eighteenth centuries knew how to mix cosmetics—an art referred to as "cosmetical physic" at the time—just as they understood how to cook, preserve, garden, and care for the sick. According to Mcgowan, cosmetic preparation was a branch of useful knowledge women were expected to master. Women often compiled their own recipe books and passed them on to their daughters.

To this day, makeup is a skill and an art we learn from and share with other women. We pass around our Bonne Bell flavoured Lipsmackers as little girls and guide each other through the application of hot pink lipstick and blue eyeliner and pass on information like "if your eyelashes don't look like tarantula legs, then you are not wearing enough mascara!" as Jennifer remembers.

"I had a real attachment to blue eyeliner and frosty pink lipstick for quite a few years," says Leah. "All the girls in my class wore the same colours: Faces #59 or #65. No matter what else you wore, it was understood that those were the hip colours to wear."

And we share tips. "My girlfriends aren't really into

makeup, so they usually ask me for tips and recommenda-tions," say Sara. "I'm obsessed with makeup and skin care, and my research and experience leaves me with the role of adviser. I love the feeling of watching my friend apply a lip pencil that I've helped her pick out. Though it's a very small thing, I know the lip pencil makes her feel more put-together and self-assured."

I love experimenting with makeup, shopping for makeup, convincing a friend to buy the newest MAC lipstick colour. Makeup is also a great way to hide that you've only had four hours' sleep, as one woman said to me.

We pride ourselves on our skills and knowledge. We learn about the different brushes, whether matte or glossy lipstick is in this season, and whether or not to line. (I don't think anyone has mastered liquid eyeliner, have they?) We enjoy the ritual. That's why we can devote an entire forum on the Bust Web site lounge (www.bust.com) to lipsticks we love. In other words, makeup is fun!

"Men have their toys—their electronics and vehicles and stuff," says Renee, the MAC makeup artist. "Women like their clothes, their shoes, and their beauty products." And like a guy who spends way too much on a new stereo with all the bells and whistles, we'll occasionally get suckered into spending $100 on a face cream that promises to remove our wrinkles, even though we know it won't.

There is an intimacy that comes from sharing this exclu-sive world. The fun of getting ready to go out at a girlfriend's house—sharing makeup and clothes—is reminiscent of that

MAKING-UP HISTORY

Egypt: 4000 B.C.

First archeological evidence of cosmetics: women applied a bright green paste of copper minerals to their faces to provide colour and definition of features.

The East: 1500 B.C.

In China and Japan, rice powder paint was used to make faces white. Eyebrows were plucked, and teeth were painted black or gold.

Greece: 1000 B.C.

Women used ochre—clay stained red with iron—as lipstick and painted their palms with henna, a red-brown dye.

Rome: c. 100 A.D.

"A woman without paint is like food without salt," wrote the Roman philosopher Plautus. The Romans used crocodile excrement for mud baths, barley flour and butter to combat pimples, and sheep fat and blood for nail polish.

14th Century

Women coated their faces with egg whites to create a glazed look and slept with slices of raw beef on their faces to get rid of wrinkles.

15th and 16th Centuries

A whitening agent for the face, composed of toxic chemicals such as lead oxide, often resulted in muscle parlysis and sometimes even death.

19th Century

Less deadly zinc oxide replaced lead oxide as a facial powder, though other poisonous chemicals were still used in eyeshadow and lip reddeners.

1915

Lipstick was first manufactured in the U.S.

1917

Theda Bara, an American actress of the silent film era, caused a sensation when she appeared on the screen heavily adorned with the cosmetics of Helena Rubinstein.

1920s

Mass makeup marketing brings red lipstick to the fore. Emergence of the chain or dime store further solidified the mass appeal of cosmetics.

1935

Max Factor opened a salon in Hollywood. Factor introduced pancake makeup, because Technicolor movies and colour television required adjustments in makeup.

1940s and 1950s

During the Second World War, leg makeup was developed in response to the shortage of stockings during the war. Ads for cosmetics and hair products appeared on television.

1960s

False eyelashes and "natural" cosmetic products become popular.

1980s

Western makeup claims to be a mélange of past styles with a new emphasis on the natural look. (Obviously not in my high school, where stripes of blush on both cheeks were anything but natural-looking!)

2000+

$45 billion to $66 billion a year is spent on cosmetics worldwide.

intimate bedroom environment we enjoyed as teenagers. Only with cocktails.

"Makeup can be a fun way to express yourself, but I'm starting to think there's something else to it," says Karen. "I recently went through a depressing period where I just felt generally blah. I did myself up with a really fun, funky look—and I wasn't even going out anywhere special. But it made me feel better, because I looked better—and it was all for me!"

But What Should I Do with My Hair?

I came across the following joke on the Internet about the difference between men and women when it comes to our hair.

Women's version:

Woman 2: Oh! You got a haircut! That's so cute!

Woman 1: Do you think so? I wasn't sure when she gave me the mirror. I mean, you don't think it's too fluffy-looking?

Woman 2: Oh God no! No, it's perfect. I'd love to get my hair cut like that, but I think my face is too wide. I'm pretty much stuck with this stuff, I think.

Woman 1: Are you serious? I think your face is adorable. And you could easily get one of those layer cuts—that would look so cute, I think. I was actually going to do that except that I was afraid it would accent my long neck.

Woman 2: Oh—that's funny! I would love to have your neck! Anything to take attention away from this two-by-four I have for a shoulder line.

Woman 1: Are you kidding? I know girls that would love to have your shoulders. Everything drapes so well on you. I mean, look at my arms—see how

short they are? If I had your shoulders I could get
clothes to fit me so much easier . . .

Men's version:

Man 1: Haircut?
Man 2: Yeah.

What can I say? Hair, like makeup, is a reflection of our
personality. Hair makes a statement. Ask any punk with a
Mohawk. And for women, yes, it's part of our packaging. We
put a lot of thought into it. We also have a lot of fun playing
with it. I used to spend hours on my Barbie's hair. I also had
one of those toy doll heads with all the hair accessories. I got
hours of enjoyment out of that. Until she too ended up with a
Mohawk, of course, which kind put a damper on my fun.

Women get very technical about hair. Like guys talking
about cars, we talk to each other about our hair. We compare
notes: Who cut it? Drugstore or professional dye job? (And
yes, unlike men who usually have no clue, women always
know whether it's a dye job or natural.) Have you ever heard
a man ask his guy friend, "What should I do with my hair?"

According to a North American survey sponsored by
Salon Selectives, 79 per cent of women ages eighteen to
twenty-eight worry about how their hair looks in public.
Forty-one per cent wish they had someone else's hair, and
38 per cent would rather be late than leave the house with
bad hair.

Granted, this report is coming from a shampoo company but the truth is, for women, a bad hair day can totally throw the planets out of whack. A study at Yale University that considered the link between hair and self-esteem said women between the ages of seventeen and thirty showed significant drops in self-esteem on bad-hair days.

I recently heard a joke about a woman who called up a female friend and was sobbing, almost unable to speak. When the woman finally calmed down enough to explain why she was so upset, her friend replied, "Oh, boy trouble. That's easy. I thought you'd got a bad haircut."

A good haircut can change your life. I remember when a dear friend of mine was going through a particularly nasty breakup. A couple of girlfriends and I decided it was time to intervene. We dragged her crushed and weepy butt to the salon and talked her into getting get her long curly locks chopped off super short. Afterwards, she looked and, more important, felt fantastic. As far as I'm concerned, dramatic post-breakup haircuts are mandatory.

And the bonus is that not only do you get a new haircut, you get a whole new wardrobe. Suddenly, clothes you never wear look great. It's fabulous. Guys just can't have this much fun with their hair.

Women's hair has always carried more symbolic value than men's. "In more superstitious days . . . people associated horror with women's hair," writes Diane Ackerman in her book *A Natural History of Love*. During the Middle Ages, the unruly hair of witches was thought to control the weather. "All manner of hail, hurricanes, or windstorms could be unleashed by a woman allowing her hair to fall wild. Of course there was always some woman somewhere who didn't give a fig for the reputed evil in her hair, and unbraided her long tresses to have a good wash. This was considered highly uncivic-minded, since, as everyone knew, a thunderstorm occurred solely because a woman somewhere was combing out her hair."

In certain cultures and religions (and among some nuns and Jewish wives), women are expected to cut their hair short or have it shaved off so that they are no longer attractive to men. Muslim women must cover their hair in public. Long hair on a woman is suggestive and implies excess, extravagance, rampant sexuality, and a lack of restraint.

Black women in North America are probably more aware than any of us of the different messages hair can send. "As black women, we do more than anyone with our hair," says the narrator in Nadine Valcin's National Film Board documentary *Black, Bold and Beautiful: Black Women's Hair*.

A black woman can choose to have her hair weaved, woolly, kinky, or nappy. She might have extensions, braids, cornrows, dreadlocks, an Afro, an updo, chinabumps, dropcurls, twists, and fingerwaves. At some point, most black women—at least in North America—face the question of whether or not to relax their hair in order to make it smooth and straight to keep up with white beauty standards.

"Back in my parents' time, it wasn't considered proper to have natural hair," says twenty-five-year-old Celeste, who remembers having her hair permed straight for the first time as a teenager. "It was like a passage into womanhood. Only children have their hair nappy and braided. It was sophisticated, ladylike, and elegant to have your hair straightened." She describes the first time she had her hair chemically treated as like undergoing an operation. She sat at the kitchen sink, surrounded by female family members with gloves on. Once again, a female beauty ritual becomes a female bonding ritual.

Tukiso remembers sitting around on Sunday evenings, listening to the radio and doing each other's hair. And twenty-nine-year-old Tammy says one of her favourite memories was watching her aunt give her grandma a perm. "When I was a kid, this was a fantastic experience, and I would make my aunt put my hair in curlers too," remembers Tammy, a freelance writer. "Then we would all have curly hairdos by evening. It was as if the old farmhouse kitchen was transformed into a hair salon for the day." Public hair salons have a long history as gathering places for women. Images of women gossiping at the local salon are all too familiar in popular culture. *Steel Magnolias*, anyone?

When men go to the barber, they're pretty much in and out. "A little off the top and sides," is about the extent of their communication. For women, it's much more complicated. "Okay, I want a cut that's short but looks long, that I can wear up or down." We need a hairdresser who understands our hair. Good communication in this relationship is as important, if not more, than in any sexual relationship we have.

That's why salons need to create a sense of intimacy says Safiya, who grew up in Nigeria and now runs her own salon in Toronto. "Putting your hair in someone else's hands makes you vulnerable," says Safiya. "I build trust with my female clients. They know I'll take care of them." As a result she says, for the twenty or thirty minutes—or eight hours if she is braiding a woman's hair—she spends with them, they feel safe and relaxed. "They open up to you about their life," says Safiya. "They'll talk to me about their relationship with their husband, their daughters or sons." Male clients, she says, are a little more reserved. "I think it's women's nature to get things out by talking. It doesn't matter what our background is, women open up to one another."

We Have Ways of Making You Talk

If you think a woman feels vulnerable having the hair on the top of her head done, imagine how vulnerable she feels with her legs spread, while someone covers her pubes with hot wax and then rips them out like a crop of dandelions.

"Women tend to reveal themselves to you," says Claudine, who has been running the Vis-à-Vis spa, which offers Brazilian, bikini, and leg waxes along with other salon treatments, in Toronto for sixteen years. Part of this, she says, is due to the spa environment. You get this cozy room to yourself, the lights are dim, there's some flaky, albeit relaxing, new-age music—everything is about comfort (okay, not the ripping your hair out by its root part). It's an environment that creates intimacy between the esthetician and the client, says Claudine. "After six months, we are like a buddy to the client. When these women come to the spa, they want to talk. I have clients who have been coming in since the day I opened. I've been seeing them since they were teenagers. I've watched them get married, become mothers, and get divorced. And I've talked them through it all. "

You have to be a bit of a therapist, she says. In fact, fifty-three-year-old Claudine, who studied her profession in her native France, says her teachers always told her that you shouldn't be an esthetician before thirty because before that age, you don't have the life experience to talk to your clients. She even knows of a Montreal spa that requires its estheticians to take a year-long sociology course before they work professionally.

Brigitte Gall, host of the television show *World's Greatest Spas*, thinks the modern version of the spa—as we experience it in North America—is like the female equivalent of going to the racetrack. For many women, it's a high, an addiction. Part of that, she says has to do with the pressure to look young. Unlike the original concept of a spa, which is based on the idea of spiritual cleansing, most North American spas now cater to helping women look young with oxygen facials, collagen implants, cellulite wraps, and, well, the list goes on.

Women, more than men, are drawn to the spa experience, says Gall, because culturally that's our safety zone. "It's a way of pushing the boys out without having to be mean," she says. "You can't actually hang a shingle outside the door that says 'No Boys Allowed,' but if the whole place is intimidating to men, then violà! We get to be pampered and not have to worry about what we look like."

According to Penny Wheelwright, director of a documentary about body hair entitled *Hair, There and Everywhere*, "We are living in the age of the 'salon culture.'" We no longer deal with hair grooming issues in the privacy of our bathroom. "Women have given over the responsibility of the care and grooming of our body hair to the waxers, threaders, laser technicians, and electrolysis experts," she says.

Hair-Raising Rituals

The issue of hair removal has always been something women bond over. Legends, stories, and traditions suggest that the waxy stick-and-yank method of hair removal dates back thousands of years. Back in Cleopatra's day, women used a hair removal process called body sugaring, a method that predates wax and uses a sugar-based product. The method reputedly was born out of a Middle Eastern bridal ritual. The night before a wedding, Lebanese, Palestinian, Turkish, and Egyptian brides had all body hair, except eyebrows and the hair on their heads, removed by the bridal party. According to lore, the bride maintained her hairless body throughout her marriage as a symbol of cleanliness and respect for her husband.

Over the years, there have been many alternative methods of hair removal, ranging from pulverized eggshells to a mixture of cat dung and vinegar.

It's no wonder Gilette's first razor designed especially for women—the Milady Décolletée—was such a hit when it came out in 1915. With skirt hems rising, smooth silky legs were the only way to go. Then, when bathing suits started creeping higher up our thighs in the sixties, even our pubic hair was no longer off limits. According to a survey by Gilette, 92 per cent of women thirteen or older in the United States shave their legs, 98 per cent shave their underarms, and 50 per cent shave their bikini line. "I think body hair is one of the last taboo subjects we have in our culture," says Wheelwright. It's one thing almost all North American women confront at some point in their lives. Should we shave, wax, use stinky goo to depilate, or have it blasted out of its follicles with electrical currents?

Most women I know started with shaving. Like makeup as a teenager, shaving your legs is another rite of passage. Most girls do it because other girls are doing it or because they've watched their mother and/or an older sister do it. I remember my friend in Grade 8 convinced me to shave my eyebrows to relieve me of my oh-so-ghastly unibrow. I was meant only to shave between the brows but got a little carried away and ended up wearing a baseball cap to school the next day to hide my botched job. By the end of the day everyone knew what had happened, and in case they didn't, our French teacher ensured they did by writing the French words for "eyebrow" and "razor" on the blackboard. I guess he thought it would be educational. I was absolutely mortified.

Most girls start with their legs rather than their eyebrows. (In fact, I don't know anyone who shaves their eyebrows, and where my friend got this idea I will never know.) Several women told me they felt "grown-up" when they shaved their legs for the first time. Some women even shaved without telling their mother and got in trouble for it. Others said they begged their mothers to let them shave. Still others say their mothers encouraged them to shave—especially when those teenage pits started to get unruly.

Shaving, like wearing makeup, makes us feel more womanly. And being an attractive woman in North American society means being hairless. When's the last time you saw a model in a fashion magazine with hairy pits? Remember the ruckus that actress Julia Roberts caused when photographers caught her with hairy underarms? Personally, I have gone through different phases in my life. At times when I've not shaved my legs or underarms, I've had to endure looks and questions.

Being hairless also seems to signify cleanliness. Which is odd, because men who don't remove their hair are not considered any dirtier than women. Yet when I crawl into bed with my hairy legs and snuggle up to my equally hairy-legged male partner, I feel uncomfortable. Several men have told me they don't mind hairy armpits or hairy legs, yet the prevalent message in our society is that a sexy woman does not have leg or armpit hair or unruly pubic hair. A friend of mine says her "quest for hairlessness" goes back to Grade 4 when a Lebanese boy—Ricky Hanna (The Banana)

—looked at her closely in natural light and said, "You should shave your moustache."

"I've never quite recovered from that," she says. "It may be something many people take for granted, but I went for about six summers never wearing shorts or skirts with bare legs." As an adult, my friend opted for electrolysis. "I finally have clean calves free of hair, but it's taken time and lots of money," she says.

While she admits that men's attitudes toward hairy women in our society have something to do with her early attempts to remove her body hair, she also feels she's "genetically predisposed to electrolysis if I want to live in a Western culture where women are allowed to show their ankles."

Which doesn't explain why women want to rip the hair off their muffs, of course. As someone who only just began to wax my bikini line a few years ago, I can barely keep up with the vulva hairstyles. Another friend of mine recently went for a Brazilian wax as a sexy anniversary gift for her beau (I've met him; he's deserving). "I thought she'd ripped my clit off!" my friend cried. Actually, at the time she really did cry. She wasn't sure who was more surprised by her new look, she or her man.

"I freaked. All I could see was a vast, hairless plain of blotchy skin. Where'd *it* go? The triangle *was* the vag for me." I'm not quite ready for that kind of hair removal commitment, though apparently plenty of women are.

"Body hair maintenance is definitely something that I obsess about since I moved to L.A.," says Kate. "It seems like in the past three years, bathing suits have gotten so tiny that everyone is completely hairless. The landing strip used to be for porn stars, and now everyone has to maintain it. How does a normal women keep up?"

Does This Make My Ass Look Huge?

Well, sometimes the "normal" woman simply doesn't keep up. It's obvious that while women take great pleasure in much of their beauty regimen, the pressure to be perfect does takes its toll.

In a poll taken in 2001 about women and body image, *People* magazine asked women whose criticism causes them the most insecurity about their bodies. Sixty-four per cent of women said the criticism was internal. Thirteen per cent came from spouses, 7 per cent from Mom and 6.5 per cent from other women.

Seventy-seven per cent of respondents said that at least half of their female friends worry about extra pounds. Obviously, women's weight concerns come in varying degrees— from the extremes of eating disorders and perpetual dieting to the less obvious ones. I don't think there is one woman on earth, no matter how thin, who hasn't suffered the occasional "fat day." At one time or another, most women hate their asses, their thighs, or feel that they are heavier than they think they should be. Certainly, much of this can be credited to a culture where thin is in and women are constantly bombarded with messages and images reminding them that their bodies are simply not good enough the way they are.

While all of this surely sucks, there is also something about our collective body self-consciousness that bonds women. We know exactly what another woman means when she says she's feeling bloated or frustrated because she had to get out her "fat pants" because she's put on ten pounds. Although a guy may just roll his eyes or tell us to get over it when we say we're feeling fat, a girlfriend will know this is merely a call for reassurance. "You look great. Don't worry," she'll say immediately. "I think you're beautiful."

Again, while some of our body image issues are no doubt fuelled by media images of what's beautiful, there is also something inherently female about dieting. Ann Kerr, who has been working with eating disordered women since 1982 (in fact, one of her first jobs was at the eating disorder clinic where yours truly was dealing with bulimia), says women have a different chemical reaction to dieting than men. "Studies have shown that when women restrict carbohydrates, it affects the tryptophan and seratonin—both mood altering chemicals—levels in their brains," says Kerr. "When men restrict carbohydrates, not much happens at all."

Women even learn how to diet together. "I remember me and my friends doing the 'jujubes diet'—this bizarre diet where you'd just eat a bag of jujubes—and we'd all get a bag and eat them together," says Kerr. Okay, she adds, so the diet would be over by dinner. Her point is that dieting is often a shared activity among women. "Dieting takes tremendous discipline, self-denial, and focus," she says. "You need a partner to support you, keep you on track, and encourage you. I think girls have always shared their secrets, their latest diet being among them."

I started my first diet when I joined my mother on the Scarsdale diet back in the seventies. "There's definitely a generation of mothers that are in the same headspace as their daughters about their bodies," says Kerr. "So we're learning it from our mothers, and the mothers are learning it from each other. Now kids have access to all sorts of media influences. They spend a lot of money on magazines that tell them what they ought to look like, so there's much more influence there, along with an exchange of information among their peer group."

It doesn't help that women are constantly admired for losing weight. "Have you lost weight?" is one of the first things we say when a woman looks good. Or that we are socialized to believe it's healthy to diet. A male friend of mine says that back in the fifties, both his mother and mother-in-law were told not to gain more than twenty-five pounds while pregnant because it would be "dangerous."

Our capacity for self-sacrifice doesn't hurt either. I was at a Christmas gathering with my mom last year and listened to her say, "Well, I shouldn't . . ." as she stuffed another hors d'oeuvre into her mouth. That's where I get it, I thought. I felt myself get angry. Just eat the damn thing if you want it! It was clear to me what messages I got about dieting when I was growing up. Food is something you enjoy guiltily. So many woman I know talk about "being good" as in, "No thanks, I'm being good" when they're passing the snacks around. It's hilarious. Only women make self-denial—in us and in other women—a bloody virtue. Kate feels as if she's lost the ability to eat anything she wants without consequence now that she lives in hyper-body-image-sensitive L.A.

Walking a Thin Line

Despite the fact that there are more opportunities for women to succeed in the world now, and even though we know more about anorexia and bulimia, dieting is more prevalent than ever. That's partly because dieting is no longer just about making ourselves appealing to men. "I think there was a time when women truly believed that taking care of themselves and maintaining their weight was about making themselves more attractive to men, but I don't think that's the case now," says Kerr. "Now I think that between women, thinness is currency. It's not enough to get married now, so competing for men isn't the only factor. Instead, women are competing with each other for a place in this world. They feel more and more pressure to prove themselves in some way." And the thing they are still most immediately rewarded for is their body.

We all know the most savage critics of women's bodies are other women. Men are usually just happy to see us naked. C'mon, admit it. You've compared yourself in the gym. You've looked at other women stuffing their faces and thought, Well, at least I'm not as bad as she is. It's hard not to compare yourself, when, as Karen says, "There are all these young hotties walking around." It's also hard not to take those insecurities out on other women.

As a result, we're conflicted. We know what's it like to go through life worrying about our bodies, and we empathize with friends who struggle with the same concerns. Again, feelings of envy and empathy battle it out in our psyche. We tell a friend she's lost weight and looks great, but if we want to lose weight ourselves, we feel a twinge of envy. When a friend complains that she's gained weight, we tell her she looks great and feel bad that she feels bad about herself, but part of us feels better, because it says, She's weak, just like me, and we can commiserate over our flaws. On top of all this is a genuine love for our friends no matter what size they are. "I think the reality is that we really don't care what our friends look like," says Karalee. "We're just concerned if they're not feeling good about themselves. We don't care if they're a size two or a size twenty, as long as they think that they're sexy. Our job is to reassure them."

It gets better as we get older. Despite the hotties, Karen admits that she's become much more secure about her body. "I genuinely like that I have curves—it feels like that's how I'm supposed to be as a woman—and for the first time, I'm glad I'm not skinny," she says. "Now when I talk to other women about my body image, it's only semi-serious stuff— like I'll joke about how I should just stick (whatever food) straight on my thighs/butt, etc."

Fashion-Conscious

A man is a person who will pay $2 for a $1 item he wants.
A woman will pay $1 for a $2 item that she doesn't want.
— SOURCE UNKNOWN

Guys are often criticized for being hung up on appearance when it comes to women. But let's be honest, women are way more hung up on other women's appearances than guys are. For example, we are all over the woman in the bad dress with the oh-so-wrong shoes.

Guys are like, hey, she's a babe. We just roll our eyes, toss each other a look, and think, Man, he just doesn't get it. Women notice details that men just don't. In the time he's managed to pull together a vague notion that the woman who just walked in the room looks okay, we've checked out her entire outfit, know whether the shoes are real Prada or knock-offs and are dying to know where she got the fabulous jacket.

It's part of the Secret Language. The way we talk to each other about our clothes connects us immediately. It's often the first thing out of my mouth when I see a friend. "Where'd you get your shoes?" "I love that top!" It's a way of saying I approve of your choices, therefore I approve of you. Women thrive on each other's approval. It lets us put our guard down a little. It's our subtle way of saying, I'm not a threat.

Because we empathize and know the pressures and struggles of trying to look good, we also share in the small victories. Like finding pants that make your stomach look flat. The way we dress is also a source of pride. I can't deny that little glow I get when another woman notices a score of mine. "Do you like it? It was marked down 70 per cent. I only paid like $80. Can you believe it!?" As if the fact that I got something for a huge discount makes it even more valuable. Men just aren't this passionate about their clothes. Well, at least most men aren't.

Admittedly, we get the whole fashion thing rammed down our throats from an early age. We learn to love clothes. Little girls are dressed in pretty outfits with matching hair baubles, little purses and other accessories. Mind you, I spent my childhood in my brother's hand-me-downs, so I don't know what my excuse is. Perhaps it was playing dress-up with my sisters. We used to wrap blankets around ourselves as dresses, cut the bottoms of Javex bottles and "fringe" the edges to make funny hats, and stuff empty thread spools in our socks to make "high heels." Hours of fun, I tell ya.

I still love to be innovative when it comes to fashion, whether hunting down unique "finds" in vintage stores or indulging in a special designer item that screams "me." I couldn't agree more with *Megatrends for Women* authors Patricia Aburdene and John Naisbitt: "When a woman's clothing accurately reflects her taste and style and flatters her body type, something clicks psychologically. She feels empowered to take on the world."

Just like there is a lipstick to suit every mood, there is an outfit to match. Each pair of black pants has a different feel; you have fat clothes and skinny clothes, take-me-serious clothes, I-be-funky clothes, and look-at-me-I am-a-hot-diva clothes. We need clothes for every mood. That's why when I go away on an overnight trip I usually bring like three bags. Hey, I know it's mid-February, but I might need that sparkly little halter top. And what if I don't feel like wearing the outfit I brought on the night of whatever occasion I brought it for? A gal needs options. And you need footwear to go with the options, which is why one of the bags is reserved exclusively for shoes. You can't wear runners with a dress, right?

According to *Megatrends*, women spend five times as much as men do on clothing. (Yet, I can stare into my bulging closet and have nothing to wear. How does this happen?) "Financial planners say women spend too much money on clothing. But for those who really love clothes, fashion is more about creativity than logic," according to Aburdene and Naisbitt. "Fashion for some women is a leisure-time activity, somewhat like spectator sports are for men. Like sports, [fashion] gets extensive media coverage. While he pores over the sports page, she might thumb through *Vogue*, *Mirabella*, or *Elle*. Many a woman considers looking at fashion the ideal way to spend a Saturday with her best friend."

Again, most of us learn the language from an early age. Tracy's mother was a shopaholic, and as a shy person, she saw clothes and shopping as a way of expressing herself. When she was young, Tracy, now thirty-four, resented her mother's love of clothes. "I always felt like she was trying to impose her taste on me, deciding what was best for me." But after years of rebellion, Tracy has learned to love clothes and shopping on her own terms. She realizes now that she and her mother still share a language when it comes to shopping. "We're both always driven to the most expensive thing in the store," she says with a laugh. "I've retained what she taught me about cuts, colours, quality of fabrics, and tailoring." Now clothes are fun for Tracy. "I like to play," she says. "I don't take it as seriously as my mother did. I define the rules, and I won't spend money somewhere that makes me feel bad or pressures me into buying something that isn't me."

According to professor emeritus Kathy Cleaver, who taught fashion history at Toronto's Ryerson University, women weren't always the only ones having fun with fashion. Until the Industrial Revolution, men also wore colourful and flamboyant clothing. Once men started to work in factories, men's clothing became conservative and remained so until

WHERE DID YOU GET YOUR SHOES!

The average American woman has twenty pairs of shoes in her closet—twice as many as the average man. What is it about women and shoes? According to Kathy Cleaver, who taught history of fashion courses at Toronto's Ryerson University, it's all about sex. "High heels throw the body a certain way so your bum sticks out and your back sways and your bust is more prominent," she says, "making a woman more sexually attractive to men. Very high heels, with minimal material on the rest of the shoe, once symbolized wantonness but now have come to signal sexual availability and attractiveness."

Sharon of Toronto's Wenches and Rogues clothing store says shoes are like the Holy Grail: "If you had the perfect pair of shoes that were comfortable and stylish, it would help you wear all those clothes in your closet."

Melanie McFarland, who wrote an article for the *Seattle Times* titled "Women and Shoes: A Love That's Felt in the Sole," tells me she's a savvy, price-conscious "shoe whore." That is, she's gotta have 'em, but they've gotta be a deal. Like the ultra-bargoon "may-wear-them-one-day" gray flannel designer heels that she "had to have" because they were reduced for quick sale from $99 to $20. McFarland recounts another tale of trying to cram her size-ten tootsies into nine-and-a-half Manolo Blahniks because they were so heavily discounted—to no avail. With the exception of winter boots, shoes are not about 'need' but, rather, desire, she says. And if you desire them badly enough, you'll just save up.

According to "Shoes That Hurt Women and the Women Who Love Them," an article by journalist Susan Okie in the *Washington Post*, "Women [in the U.S.] visit orthopedic surgeons for foot problems four times as often as men, and they undergo about 87 per cent of operations performed to correct acquired foot deformities, such as bunions and hammer toes. In societies where people go barefoot or wear flat sandals, acquired foot deformities in adults are rare and their frequency is the same in both sexes."

Women on Shoes

My mom told me a long time ago that if you go into a really nice store and you want good service, you should wear good shoes. I was shopping with friends recently and we went into several exclusive designer shops and one thing we noticed was that the salespeople would say hi, look at our bags, then look at our shoes. In one place, the woman barely spoke to us because our stuff wasn't nice enough. – Christine, 33

Shoe concern starts in school. When we were kids, you were cool if you wore your Cougar boots or Adidas (but only in the right colour) with the laces untied. We were dead scared of ridicule when Mom would come home with the cheap Sears knock-offs. – Marie, 35

In high school, we had these Le Château elfin shoes that came to the most severe point about three inches out from the end of our big toe, and we'd always trip over our own feet and slide across the ice, but they were part of our 'uniform,' and we didn't care if we died as a result. – Catherine, 37

One time my friend pulled over to us in her car and she was like 'Look what I got at Nordstrom! I got them for $80!' and they were Manolo Blahniks! I just wanted to reach into the car and strangle her. To this day we all tell the story of the Blahniks, like it was this great war, this epic battle, won. – Melanie, 28

I come from multiple generations of shoe lovers. In fact, my grandmother (probably the only eighty-five-year-old in her nursing home who still wears leather) has problems with her feet as a result of years of wearing shoes with serious heels. Whenever I go home to visit my parents, my mother always sits me down to show off her new purchases. – Tracy, 34

I don't care if my shoes are comfortable. I bought a really high-heeled pair, and by the end of the first night wearing them out, my friend literally had to hold me up so I could make it to a cab. My knees hurt for a week after, but I had lots of compliments on them, so it almost made the pain worthwhile. – Rebecca, 28

I hold myself differently depending on the style of shoe I'm wearing. I am by no means athletic, but when I wear my Pumas, I feel like I could kick some major ass.
    – Sue, 31

MEMORABLE MOMENTS IN SHOE HISTORY

4000 B.C.
> Earliest depictions of shoes (flexible leather pieces held in place with lacings) appeared in ancient Egyptian murals on tombs and temples.

1000 A.D.
> At Saxon weddings, the father of the bride customarily presented the groom with one of the bride's shoes, symbolizing transfer of his authority over her. The bride's shoe was thrown to the bridesmaids; the one who caught it would be next to marry.

Early 1500s

The high heel was invented, possibly by Leonardo da Vinci.

Mid-1500s

Chopines, platform shoes rising up to thirty inches, became all the rage in southern Europe.

Late 1700s

Marie Antoinette ascended the scaffold to be executed wearing two-inch heels. However, in the wake of the French Revolution, heels became lower than at any time in the eighteenth century.

Late 1800s

Buttonhooks became an essential part of every woman's wardrobe as high-buttoned shoes were the fashion norm.

1900–1910

People developed a preference for narrow feet, believed to be a sign of breeding and gentility. Both men and women regularly wore shoes a full size too small. Some women opted to have their little toes removed to achieve "the look."

1920s

With shorter skirts, the foot became a focal point of fashion. Shoe styles, now mass-produced, were reinfluenced by crazes like the Charleston, a dance that demanded a securely fastened shoe with a low heel and closed toe.

1930s

Designers experimented with shoe fashion, creating platform shoes from wood, cork, and other materials due to a shortage of leather and a war ban on rubber.

1940s

Overseas, leather was restricted to military use, so shoe designers incorporated reptile skins and mesh. Cork or wood-soled "wedgies" were another staple. Women everywhere used household items, including cellophane and pipe cleaners, to create festive shoe decorations.

1950s

The girl with low and sensible heels is likely to pay for her bed and meals. – Saturday Evening Post

The post-war boom provided a sense of economic optimism and led to increased consumerism. Constant rounds to barbecues, cocktail parties, and other social events required dressing up. The stiletto heel was developed in 1951.

1960s

With miniskirts and hot pants, it was an era of "anything goes"—from iridescent rainbow platforms to classic colonial or Edwardian-style pumps and go-go boots. A leather shortage and the space-age craze inspired shoes in new materials such as vinyl and plastic.

1970s

Designers took platform heels to new heights, building seven to eight-inch stacked heels (and covering them in all manner of adornments) for customers such as Elton John, David Bowie, and Cher. The film *Saturday Night Fever* created massive demand for strappy platform heels for women.

1980s

"It's harder to climb the ladder of success in high heels" was a common sentiment. Some women began dressing in mannish simplicity—including flats and low-heeled shoes—while attempting to shatter the glass ceiling.

1990s and beyond

Diversity is key. Whether it's heavy, whimsical, clunky, or dainty, it's out there.

about the sixties. At the same time, women were stuck at home with nothing much else to do but look good. This became a bit of a status symbol, says Cleaver. "The better your wife looked and the more frivolous, impractical clothes she could wear, the wealthier one appeared."

Not surprisingly, this was also about the time when shopping became a favourite female pastime, an activity we often experience with our gal pals.

Shop Till You Drop

The word "shop" as a noun has been traced back as far as the fourteenth century. But its use as a verb, as in "I love shopping!" didn't show up until the late 1700s.

According to a 1998 *New York Times* article by Sarah Boxer titled "I Shop, Ergo I Am: The Mall as Society's Mirror," the word "shopping" started to appear frequently in print around 1780 in England. "At that point, the usual morning employment of English ladies," the eighteenth-century writer Robert Southey said, "was to 'go a-shopping.' Stores became places to socialize, to see and be seen. Browsing was born." Shopping became defined as a female activity, and unlike many traditional female activities, one that took place outside the home—gasp—in public. In other words, it got us out of the bloody house.

Under the traditional division of labour at the time, "the shopping" became part of a woman's domestic chores. At the time, women constituted between 70 and 95 per cent of all shoppers and spent three times as much as men. Shops exploited this by creating "female-friendly" environments and appealing to women's desires with promises that certain products could offer us a certain way of life. Suddenly shopping was about fulfilling, or at least dreaming about fulfilling, our fantasies.

"If, as individuals, women had little influence in the world of business," writes Boxer, "in the marketplace she collectively called the shots. Shopping gave women a good excuse to sally forth, sometimes even in blissful solitude, beyond the clutches of family. It was the first form of women's liberation, affording an activity that lent itself to socializing with other adults, clerks and store owners and fellow shoppers."

It's also a great way to deal with stress. Nothing like a little retail therapy to get you through a rough spot. Recently at a party I ran into a woman from England who was going through a difficult time in her marriage. She had flown over to stay with an old friend in Montreal for a week to help clear her head. The night I ran into her, she had just spent the day shopping and was positively glowing.

"I hit the shops, dropped like $200 in an hour, and that was just in one area of town," she told me excitedly. I was thrilled because she had discovered one of my favourite designer stores.

"They have an outlet store," I gushed, and shared my secret discovery. We spent the next hour swapping shopping stories and strategies and, by the time she left the party, we were buds.

As far as I'm concerned, shopping is an art, and women who are into it know this. We take great pride in our ability to find good bargains or something unique that we feel communicates who we are. "I think that on some level, we buy a statement and then hope to God and Vishnu that that will be enough," says Brigitte Gall. "A Prada bag says a great deal about you—in the right circles."

Of course, she adds, "a Prada bag can't tell a joke, make you humble or stick up for you when some crusty co-worker decides to make your life a living hell. But if I wear my Nike runners, a Gap jersey, and drive an SUV, without even having to open my mouth, I've told you that I am a woman who Just Does It, leading a carefree but active life, and for once in my life, can be equal in stature to a man."

Paying for Pleasure

But women don't shop just to make statements. For women, shopping is an oportunity to bond with other women. "Women like to shop with friends, egging each other on and rescuing each other from ill-advised purchases," says Paco Underhill, retail anthropologist and author of *Why We Buy*. "I don't think we'll ever see two men set off on a day of hunting for the perfect bathing suit."

Sophie Kinsella captures the joy of shopping brilliantly in her novel *Confessions of a Shopaholic*, the story of a woman who can't stop shopping, even as she sinks further and further into debt. In an online interview, she describes the almost therapeutic pleasure women get from shopping. "I just think people get a real buzz from going into a shop and seeing the exact thing they want. It's like going to a party, seeing a guy you like and thinking, I want that."

"Only with shopping," she says, "you can have it—that's the difference. When you see a man that you like, you have to sidle up to him and practice your chat-up lines, and wait to see if he calls you. It's all extremely stressful. But with a pair of shoes, that's it—you pick them off the rack, try them on, and if you want them, they're yours in an instant. It's the ultimate power. Complete control. It's like the pursuit of pleasure." And these days, she adds, because women are financially independent they don't have to worry about "spending the housekeeping." We all work really hard, and shopping is a way of rewarding our efforts. It's a feel-good activity.

As Katherine, a twenty-six-year-old medical student, said to me, problems seem smaller when you're looking fantastic in a little black dress.

Lesa, a twenty-eight-year-old assistant editor at a fashion magazine, agrees. She was taught by her mother not to resist a bargain. "Even if I have no money, it's fun to look, to get inspired and to scope out what to look for when it goes on sale."

"Shopping is relaxing," says Claire, who has worked for several years at the Toronto store of Wenches and Rogues, a designer clothing chain. Claire got her interest in clothing from her mother, whom she describes as creative with impeccable taste. She used to take Claire and her three sisters shopping. They still shop when they're all together. Like Kinsella, Claire gets a buzz from shopping. "It is a bit of a drug to be able to find something and take it home and admire it and wear it," says Claire. "And for some women it's like therapy. As women we're inundated with the idea of being pretty, so if we're having a bad day, we'll go shopping." Claire says her best experience selling clothes so far was having a client tell someone at a cocktail party that "Claire's great. She made me love my ass."

"That made me feel so good," says Claire. "I don't just sell clothes. I talked this woman down. We should get some honorary psychology certificate!"

We all know that shopping when you don't feel good about yourself is self-torture. If you don't end up running out of the shop in tears, you inevitably buy stuff you don't want and that will hang in your closet unworn, forever reminding you of that bad day. But a new outfit can also turn a day around. Claire's colleague, Sharon, says some female clients will come in for an outfit before a big meeting because they need something to make them feel more powerful. "It's like putting on a costume," says Sharon, who remembers stealing the outfits from her brother's Batman doll and putting them on her Barbie.

"One season you can buy all sorts of black pants and dark lipsticks and cool shades and turn into a mysterious urban woman who wants to be left alone," adds Devalina. "And then the next season you can choose berry-type kissable shades and sexy tank tops when you want some attention."

Yes, we want attention. While we love it when other women admire our taste, we don't mind at all if the boys notice. "It's more important to you if your boyfriend goes 'Wow,' right?" asks Sharon. "If you're wearing something new and he says, 'I never noticed that your ass looks so great,' that means so much more than your girlfriend going 'Cute dress. Where'd you get that?'"

I don't know. I've even taught my boyfriend to ooh and ahh appropriately when I come home and show off my scores, but somehow it's not quite the same as having my girlfriends gush when I tell them I paid only seven bucks for my fabulous second-hand leather jacket. But it does in a pinch. That said, I suppose I do like it when he notices something new without me having to mention it. But girlfriends always notice.

I love shopping with girlfriends. You need them to be honest with you when a saleswoman is telling you something looks fab when you think it looks like shite. Or to run and grab sizes, or to get you to try things on that you might not otherwise, and to help you rationalize that way-too-expensive dress by convincing you of all the use you'll get out of it.

But you have to go with the right friends. Sharon says things can sometimes get ugly when women shop together. "Some women play out their bitterness or their jealousies on their friends," she says. "They'll cut each other down, or say something doesn't look good when it does. Or you'll see one woman eating it up while her friend tells her how fabulous she looks. Meanwhile, you can tell it's making her feel like shit about herself."

That's why, sometimes, you gotta shop solo—especially when you're on a mission for a specific item or if you're in a second-hand store. A friend and I drove in silence for an hour after fighting over a hat we found at a second-hand shop we stopped at while on a road trip.

"I like thrift stores because they're cheap," says Margaret. That way if you decide you look heinous in those banana-yellow bell bottoms, you won't feel guilty about giving them away again. They are also more of a challenge. "I get a secret sense of pride when people compliment me on my great new coat or my wonderful sense of style because I know that my two hours of hunting through acid-washed jeans and stained Ts paid off," says Margaret. "And there are wonderful, well-made little mod dresses I've found at thrift stores that I'd never find in any department store."

But shopping isn't always fun. Sometimes, when everything is like size two, or you try on a pair of pants that are two sizes bigger than you usually take and they're tight because sizes are completely wonky these days (I mean, what the hell is size zero about anyway?), it can do a number on you. That's why Rachel hates shopping. "I have a strangely shaped body," she says. "I have an incredibly small waist and large thighs. Finding clothes is next to impossible, and I never feel good about my body when I leave a store."

And for Claire, who has to be in this environment for seven hours a day, it can be toxic. "Some days when I'm feeling really bad myself, I find it hard to be in the store," she admits. "Women are constantly comparing themselves to you. Or they'll put on something I've got on and it looks better on them. It can be rough if you're feeling insecure."

Born to Shop?

I can't imagine a guy feeling bad cause his friend looks so hot in those pants he just tried on. It's not a big secret that guys don't shop like gals. Claire notices the difference in her store, which carries men's and women's clothing. "There are some guys that genuinely love clothes," she says, "but for most men, it's about efficiency."

According to Paco Underhill, 65 per cent of men who take jeans into a dressing room will buy them, while only 25 per cent of women will. (No doubt some of this has to do with the horrible lighting and weird mirrors they install in women's changing rooms. Hello, people, are you trying to sell us stuff or scare us?) Also, while 86 per cent of women look at price tags when they shop, only 72 per cent of men do. "For a man, ignoring the price tag is almost a measure of his virility," writes Underhill. After observing men and women shopping, Underhill also discovered that a woman shopping with a man will spend less time (four minutes, forty-one seconds) in a store than if shopping alone (five minutes, two seconds), or with a friend (eight minutes, fifteen seconds), or even with a child (seven minutes, nineteen seconds).

On their own, women are the most efficient shoppers. When two women shop together, they talk, advise, suggest, and consult with each other. With kids, you gotta keep them under control and entertained. That's much easier than keeping a guy entertained, one who usually makes it clear that he's bored within thirty seconds.

Women like to take their time looking, comparing prices, and checking out the entire store. I even do this at the grocery store. I often get frustrated when I'm with the guy and he's heading right for the aisles that contain the stuff he knows he wants. I prefer to go aisle by aisle, because who knows what unknown treasures they may hold?

"Women generally care that they do well in even the smallest act of purchasing," says Underhill, "and they take pride in their ability to select the perfect thing, whether it's a cantaloupe or a house or a husband." Observe a man in the produce section, he suggests. A guy will grab a head of lettuce off the top of the pile and off he goes, brown, rotten leaves or not, without even glancing at the price. A woman will carefully pick through the entire pile until she finds the perfect lettuce. And she will definitely check the price. Interestingly, while I am like this with clothes and food, my guy is like this with certain items—like records, for example. "Men do take pride in their proficiency with certain durable goods—cars, tools, boats, barbecue grills, computers," admits Underhill.

But even so, the boys still don't have the same psychological and emotional relationship to shopping that women do. "Men will go out and buy loads of stuff all at once," says

Confessions of a Shopaholic author Sophie Kinsella. "I was speaking with this guy last week who told me that he had done his year's shop in one day. He was into designer clothes, but he just went out and bought them all in one hit." The trouble with her, she says, is that she could do all that, but it wouldn't last. "I'll see something else and do it all again a couple of weeks later. It's like an appetite. You eat loads and loads of food and think you'll never eat again, and the next day it's like 'Okay, what's for breakfast?'"

"I think women like to shop more than men because we buy into the belief that we actually might find that one item that will correct all of our flaws and make us look gorgeous," says Bethany. "Men aren't fed that same fool's gold message of perfection." Because women are judged so harshly on their appearance, shopping becomes another way of "fitting in." Purchasing the right clothes, shoes, or makeup as an adult is like wearing the right clothes in high school to fit in.

Guys that do love shopping as much as women do are usually fashion-conscious. Though most guys aren't trained in this the way women are. "I think when men know what looks good on them, they learn to love shopping, because they realize what a great boost it is to your self-esteem to be able to make yourself look good," says Kimberly.

Funny that as women's lives have changed to become more like men's—with more focus on career and less on family—so have our shopping habits. More and more, says Underhill, women are evolving into male hit-and-run shoppers instead of dedicated browsers and searchers. While women

SHOPPING RULES

- Never shop with a thin friend on a "fat day."

- Never shop on a "fat day."

- If you're over sixteen, and you and a friend want to buy the same thing, make sure you
    - a) live in different cities;
    - b) promise to call each other before wearing said item to an event you will both be attending;
    - c) don't comment on how concerned you are that said item makes your tummy bulge/thighs look big/breasts sag when other friend has bulgier tummy/bigger thighs/saggier breasts.

- You must have no more than three items in your closet still bearing price tags.

- You must pay bills before shopping unless you have
    - a) just been dumped;
    - b) just been fired;
    - c) got a lousy haircut that an outfit might help fix;
    - d) got a great haircut that absolutely needs a new outfit to go with it.

- Never trust dressing room mirrors. As much as you'd like to believe it, you haven't suddenly gained five inches on your legs or got a fabulous tan since entering the store. (This is why we bring good friends who will tell us the truth.)

- If shopping with friends, never interrupt a good trawl by whining and asking, "Can we go now?" We'd shop with guys if we wanted that.

- If a friend says she likes something that you think is absolutely awful, do not express your disapproval by pointing and laughing at her horrendous taste. Simply say something like "Hmmm . . . you think so? It's not my style," then quickly get it out of her sight by suggesting something better.

- If you are shopping with someone less "flush" than you, avoid ridiculously overpriced boutiques, and do not say things like "$300 actually isn't a bad price for these pants. Can you hang on to them while I have a quick look at this rack of cashmere sweaters?"

may have more money than women of previous generations did, we have less time to spend it.

That's not to say we'll ever give up shopping as a leisure activity. Stores know this. More female-friendly environments have emerged in traditionally male shopping zones. Hardware stores like Home Depot are a good example of this. "Instead of displaying a box of bathroom faucets, stores now show the whole tub, complete with shower curtain and towels," writes Underhill. Before, you went to a hardware store only when you needed something. Now, you go just to browse, to see what's new and what's on display.

Cosmo Girls?

I have to say the one time my conscious, careful consumerism goes out the window is when I buy fashion magazines. After all that exacting grocery shopping, I'm at the checkout counter and next thing you know I've got copies of *Cosmo*, *Glamour*, and *InStyle* in my cart. I know the "52 Ways to Make Him Lust After You Forever" article is going to say exactly the same thing as last month's "How to Make Him Want Your Bod Now!" I know the ridiculously skinny models are gonna drive me nuts. Yet I'm too weak to resist. I can hardly wait to get home, draw a nice warm bath, fix myself a drink, and sink in for some good, solid trashy reading, and lots of great fashion and makeup ideas that I'll promise myself I'll try but somehow I never actually get around to.

My other favourite way to enjoy women's mags is with a bunch of gal pals, preferably during some out-of-town adventure, in a cabin somewhere where we drink cocktails ("pussytails" or "clittails," as we prefer to call them) and read aloud all the wackiest and most outrageous stuff we can find. This might launch a discussion about sex and whether we've tried some of this stuff. Then we complain to each other about the ridiculously skinny models and coo over the fabulous clothes, makeup, and hair.

Women's magazines: we love to hate them and we hate
to love them. We hate them because, as one woman put it,
"They are full of a bunch of man-pleasing bullshit and everyone is a size two with beautiful hair, perfect skin, a flat stomach, and excellent teeth." We hate that they prey on our
insecurities to make us buy all the products they advertise.

"I read *Glamour* yesterday," says Mahalia, a thirty-two-
year-old graphic designer, "and it seemed that on every page
there was something brand-new that I needed to fix about
myself: get rid of those bags under your eyes; lose your gut;
your ass is too big; your hair is not shiny; there is too much
hair around your vagina; you have blackheads on your chin;
there is acne on your chest; your breasts are too floppy; and
on top of all this someone is trying to steal your man." Of
course, we still buy magazines by the truckload. (That *Glamour* that makes us feel not so glamorous has a circulation of
2.2 million.) Not without guilt, mind you.

Most of the women I talked to who said they liked
women's magazines almost always followed up their praise
with a "but. . . ." "I buy them, but I feel guilty and silly about
it," says nineteen-year-old Erin, who is a student. "I like to
rip on the skinny models with my girlfriends—it makes us
feel better about ourselves."

Women's magazines are such an easy target for all that is
wrong with our society. While we like to complain that they
promote anorexia and make us dissatisfied and upset with
ourselves because we can't afford the clothes and everything
else they're hawking, they are chick-oriented and promote

independence and strong women. Most of the time they're saying, Go out and get what you want and here's the outfit you can wear to do it.

"They don't make me insecure because I'm very conscious that it is a fabricated world," says Sarah, thirty-six, a long-time fashion magazine junkie. "I might think in passing, I wanna look like that, but it doesn't destroy my self-esteem." For Sarah, fashion magazines are a shallow indulgence. "It's like watching *Entertainment Tonight*," she says. "It's my downtime. Plus I like knowing what's hip."

Women's mags keep us in the fashion loop. They teach us how to talk about clothes. How did you learn what a shrug or a pashmina shawl was? Thanks to fashion magazines, these things become part of our lexicon, and other women know exactly what we're talking about, while men scratch their heads trying to figure out the difference between a mule, a flat, and a slingback. We share what's in them with each other. You'd never hear a guy say to his buddy, "Oh hey, did you see those boots in *GQ*?"

Our mags provide inspiration. "I love fashion," continues Sarah. "These magazines give me ideas and cues about what's in style. I'll look at pictures and rip out ones of clothes I'd like to make." But even Sarah admits that sometimes, "If I'm feeling frumpy and gross, I'm like 'Fuck you!'"

In *Consuming Subjects: Women, Shopping, and Business in the Eighteenth Century*, Susan Douglas articulates the ambivalence women have toward these magazines. "When I open *Vogue*, for example, I am simultaneously infuriated and seduced, grateful to escape temporarily into a narcissistic paradise where I'm the centre of the universe, outraged that completely unattainable standards of wealth and beauty exclude me and most of the women I know from the promised land. I adore the materialism; I despise the materialism. I yearn for the self-indulgence; I think self-indulgence is repellent. I want to look beautiful; I think wanting to look beautiful is the most dumb-ass goal you could have. The magazine strokes my desire; the magazine triggers my bile."

Women's magazines weren't always this much fun. During the seventeenth century, women were largely excluded from the world of journalism, though women had a small but not negligible presence in the periodical press. When the *Journal des Dames* came out in France in 1759, it was the first magazine to make the bold commitment "par et pour les dames" (by and for women). According to Nina Rattner Gelbart in *A History of Women in the West: Renaissance and Enlightenment Paradoxes*, the *Journal* was originally conceived by its male founder as "an innocuous bauble to amuse society ladies at their toilette." However, from 1761 to 1775, a succession of three female editors transformed it into a serious oppositional publication addressing social issues, preaching reform, and challenging its readers to think, to "abandon vanity, and to feed their minds."

By the 1790s, a number of publications devoted to fashion began to appear, with reports of what was being worn by court ladies in London and Paris. Forging the link between femininity and clothing, fashion became a staple of women's magazines for the next two hundred years. By the turn of the twentieth century, women's mags were cheap, mass-produced, and nationally distributed, meaning most women could buy them and share them with their friends. According to Alex Kuczynski in a 1999 *New York Times* article titled "Ideas and Trends: Enough About Feminism. Should I Wear Lipstick?" when Edward Bok assumed the editorship of the *Ladies' Home Journal* in 1889, it was an established periodical with a circulation of 440,000. By 1893, this figure went up to 700,000 and by 1904 rose to one million. Later in the twentieth century, *LHJ* was followed by a whole new crop of women's magazines including *Woman's Home Companion*, *Good Housekeeping*, and *Harper's Bazaar*. In the seventies and eighties, magazines such as *Glamour* ran serious articles like "Let's Stop Lying About Day Care," and "Excuse Me, Are Women Equal Yet? 18 Reasons Why We Still Need Affirmative Action." But by January of 1999, *Glamour* had dropped its "Women in Washington" column, which covered political activity concerning women's issues, and re-placed it with an astrology column. And still circulation figures rose. *Marie Claire* has gone from a circulation of 400,000 in 1996 to more than double that in 2002.

"Editors also know that while women may complain about the tyranny of unattainable bodies, aspirational images still sell magazines," writes Robin Pogrebin in a 1997 *New York Times* article titled "Adding Sweat and Muscle to a Familiar Formula." In that piece, Pogrebin quotes Lesley Jane Seymour, the editor-in-chief of *YM* (*Young Miss*), who says: "The girls on the front of the magazine have to be prettier, something to aspire to. Readers may say they want more reality, but when you give them more reality, it doesn't sell."

Bonnie Fuller, a Canadian and former editor-in-chief of *Cosmo* says, "I don't think women are buying magazines to look at their next-door neighbours. Women enjoy fantasy. It's genetic." Magazine history doesn't exactly encourage risk-taking, either, when it comes to women's publications. Feminist *Ms.* magazine, for example, has a circulation of 200,000 compared with *Good Housekeeping* (4.6 million), *Seventeen* (2.5 million) and *Vogue* (1.1 million). Not bad for something so many women claim to hate.

Gloria Steinem, the feminist writer who helped found the twenty-five-year-old *Ms.* magazine has said that women's magazines can't venture too far off the beauty and fashion formula because fashion and beauty advertisers account for up to 95 per cent of the advertising space in these magazines. Consequently, Ms. stopped accepting ads in 1990. But many editors say that if a lot of beauty and fashion still occupies their pages, it's because readers want it that way. In 1997 alone, buyers of women's magazines spent $52 billion on apparel and about $4 billion on cosmetics.

While there is certainly something to be said about how these magazines keep women consuming, I still maintain there is a guilty pleasure associated with them that goes beyond being duped by their messages. I know I won't have a bust that never sags or men panting at my feet thanks to some sex tips I picked up from *Cosmo*. Naomi Wolf, author of

The Beauty Myth, describes women's magazines as simultaneously oppressive of women while at the same time being one of the only female forms of mass culture. I tend to agree. I think women love these magazines as one of the few places where we can indulge in a world completely devoted to us, even if it's not exactly us, and even if a lot of it is annoying and bogus. After all, a lot about being a woman is annoying and bogus. These magazines help us look at it all and laugh about it—while secretly indulging in it. Their promises of transformation take us back to wanting to be princesses on the schoolyard. We are comfortable in their contractions because we've lived our entire lives with contradiction.

In *A Magazine of Her Own?*, Margaret Beetham talks about women's magazines evolving—much as the nineteenth-century middle-class home did—into a "feminized space." Like the home, these magazines are defined by the women who are at their centre and by their difference from the masculine world of politics and economics. "It did not necessarily empower women," writes Beetham. "However, the woman's magazine, like other 'feminized spaces,' including women's studies courses, hen parties, and girls' schools, also has a radical potential. . . . It may become a different kind of feminized space, one in which it is possible to challenge oppressive and repressive models of the feminine."

In a way, these magazines give us opportunity to be critical of ourselves and of the social pressure placed upon us in a language that is our own. Beetham argues that the writing style of women's mags is similar to how women communicate with one another—the chatty gossipiness, the breaking up of the text into snippets, the colloquialisms, and the creation of journalistic and editorial personae that address the reader as an intimate friend.

"Fashion, domestic advice, mini-biographies of the Royal Family, interviews with celebrities, all were subsumed into the general category of 'chat.' The magazine therefore represented itself not only as a repository of womanly wisdom, which it passed on to 'Young Mothers and New Housewives,' but also as the place in which women shared with each other the secrets of their femininity."

Keeping It Together

"Oh my God, I was just gonna call you!" How many times have you heard yourself shriek this into the phone when a girlfriend you haven't heard from in a while suddenly calls? It's almost creepy, isn't it? You feel like a phony saying, "Wow, I was just thinking of you this morning," but you really, really were. It's like some female sixth sense goes off when too much time has passed since the last time you talked and you know it's time to reconnect.

Let's face it, female friendships take a beating as we grow older and life takes us in different directions. Unlike during childhood or high school when we spend every free second with our girlfriends, as we mature, careers, relationships, kids, and other life changes make it harder and harder to keep these friendships alive. As much as we hate it, we have to start "scheduling" our friends. "My friends have all gone separate ways with their lives," says Fawn, a thirty-year-old public relations director. "My good friend has a son and is pregnant with her second child. We have breakfast almost every Saturday at a cheap diner near her house. By scheduling a regular time, we stay connected."

And because we have to put a little more effort into staying connected, this is the time we start to weed out the friends that aren't worth that effort. The tier system starts to take hold.

Tier One consists of those two or three girlfriends who are like gold. These are the women that have been there for the long haul—the inner circle. These women fuel you and make you feel connected to your past and equipped for the future. These are the gals who have seen you at your best and worst. They know and love you, no matter what. You can have a pee while on the phone with them. Contact consists of several phone calls (not all of them while peeing) or e-mails a week, plus, if all planets are aligned, at least one face-to-face encounter, maybe a weekend night, even if you're in a relationship.

Tier Two includes the women you love dearly, but just don't have the chance to see or talk to daily or even weekly. I recently got together with three of my favourite Tier Two friends. During university, we saw each other almost every day and spent hours around one of our kitchen tables talking, drinking wine, making dinner, and holding banana blow job contests. These girls made university fun. After school, a couple of us moved to different cities. One of us had kids. We kept in touch, phoning or e-mailing several times a year.

These days, we're all in the same city again and make a point of getting together at least once or twice a year for birthdays or before Christmas. What I love most about these women is that although we may not talk for months, we can pick things up right where we left off. The moment we are all in the same room together, we are a bundle of energy and excitement. "Wow, I love your hair!" "Where did you get those pants—they're fantastic!" Within seconds we are on to the details of one another's lives as well as the lives of people we know in common. We talk about relationship problems, who's pregnant, who's getting married. We compare our sex lives and talk about how hot one of us looked at a recent work party. The intimacy is immediate, enormously satisfying and invigorating.

Even though you know you can pick up where you left off—even if you haven't talked to these friends for months or years—ideally you don't want to let too much time pass before getting in touch with Tier Two friends. Luckily, that sixth sense usually starts tingling when you know it's time to pick up the blower, fire off an e-mail, or arrange a karaoke night.

Tier Three consists of friends of convenience—your kids go to the same daycare, her husband or boyfriend is your husband or boyfriend's best friend, you work together, and so on. Tier Three friends can sometimes become temporary or even permanent Tier One friends as you find yourself spending more time with these women than your usual Tier One group because of life circumstances. One must be careful, however, not to entirely abandon original Tier One friends for new Tier Three friends. After all, Tier One friends will still be there when the relationship/kids/career is not.

Tier Four friendships are the friends you see once in a while, ones you know through a friend of a friend. You like each other but you don't necessarily share all the gritty details of your lives. Tier Four is where some of the more troublesome female friendships live. These are the women you have befriended over the years whom you like on some level but who can be overly demanding or emotionally needy. Sure, we tend to rely on each other for emotional support, but there have to boundaries. The constantly needy or constantly in crisis are draining. Especially if the emotional exchange only goes one way. A good sign of this is when someone you consider a Tier Four friend considers you her Tier One friend. These are the ones who expect to hear from you more than they do. These can become what are known as the "high-maintenance" friends. And, as a result, Tier Four friends can turn into Tier Five friends.

Tier Five friends are bottom-feeders. These are the ones whose calls you let go to voice mail, the ones you just can't shake. The ones you feel obligated to drag your ass out to dinner with and spend the night listening to their problems because they have no one else to talk to. Female friendships are way too demanding to put energy into the ones that aren't worth it. As we get older, life gets in the way and forces us to prioritize. Of course, despite having our friendships neatly organized and categorized, sometimes even the best Tier One friendships can't withstand life's changes.

As much as we'd like to control every decision a friend makes, there are bound to be a few things she's going to do that we don't necessarily agree with. And that can put a strain on the relationship. Depending on the extent of the strain, sometimes things get ugly and you have to have "the talk."

My male friends are always amazed at the emotional complexity of my female friendships. The idea of getting together with any of their male friends to discuss the state of their friendship simply baffles men. But the truth is that because of the depth of what we share and the importance of feeling connected, my close female friendships can sometimes feel as—if not more—complex than my romantic relationships. And at times, as much as you try and try to talk it through, you may reach the point where you have to accept that your friendship has changed. And then decide whether to let the friendship drift or find a new way to enjoy it. We can only hope that one day our old friendship will return to the way it was. Sometimes it never does.

Losing a good friend can be even more sad and heart-breaking than breaking up with a man. There's always another man out there. But as we get older, we're less sure that we'll be able to create the friendship bond with another woman, one who doesn't know our history, hasn't been there through all the other men, and can't just hang out the way we like to.

Losing an old friend also means you have to let go of that fantasy you shared when you were single that you would all grow old in a big house together.

Friends and Lovers

This is why we take it so hard when a girlfriend abandons friendship for a relationship. "What's worse," says Margaret, "are those girlfriends who are your best friend when they're single but as soon as they meet the girl or guy of their dreams, they're like 'Oh, I think s/he's the one. See ya.' And you never hear from them.'" That is, of course, until they come crawling back like a month later with their heart shattered to smithereens wanting you to help them lick the wounds.

I mean, sure, relationships take up a lot of time, but you always have to remember the girlfriend rules and make sure you make time with your girls a regular priority. "I rarely date and female friendships have always been *the* most important relationships in my life," says Suzanne. "It's sad that as we get older, we let men replace the importance of our girlfriends, because really, those two types of relationships serve completely different purposes. I've seen our circle of friends slowly diminish as more and more of our girlfriends allow their boyfriends to dominate their lives—and it isn't always the boyfriend's fault."

Yes, we've all done it at some point. We isolate ourselves in a new relationship, thinking this person is giving us everything we need, and then, when it all goes to hell in a handbasket, we realize there's no one around to catch us when we fall. Then we have to sheepishly go crawling back to all the friends we've been neglecting and work ourselves back into their favour. I try not to make a habit of this, and my girls know this, so the few times I've fallen into this trap, they've taken me back into the fold. It's the friends who do this every time who are pushing their luck.

However, the smart ones learn that through everything that life serves us, the one constant is female friendships. Luckily most of us are pretty smart. According to studies done by Claire A. Etaugh and Judith S. Bridges and cited in their book *The Psychology of Women*, women, more than men, retain separate friendships after marriage, despite the prevailing notion that women ultimately seek out relationships to fulfill all their emotional needs. "While men usually choose their wife as their confidant, women generally turn to each other to confide their innermost feelings, their joys, miseries, and problems," write the authors. "More than men, women lead separate emotional lives after marriage."

That's because even though we may decide to share our life with a guy, he still doesn't get us the way our female friends do. For example, while I was writing this book, my guy was wonderfully supportive. He gave me great advice. But at times when I was really struggling, he found it hard to know how to comfort me. In most cases, he'd get more freaked out about my emotional state, and next thing I'd know, I'd be consoling him about how my being upset upset him. How screwed up is that?

While his first instinct was to try to fix whatever problem I was having, my girlfriends just let me vent, offered me sympathy, and suggested some parallel to a similar experience from their own lives. Then they'd crack a joke that would send me into a fit of giggles and we'd go off on a tangent about something completely unrelated that would take my mind off my problems. The conversations always calmed me down. I felt understood, loved, and comforted.

Also, if we didn't have girlfriends outside our romantic relationships, who would we bitch to about our partners? Our need to talk about relationships doesn't go away just because we get married or enter a long-term relationship. In many ways we need this more as we chart the unfamiliar territory of long-term commitment. When we were all single and dating, it was easy to commiserate with each other about what jerks men were and pat each other on the back about how we were right and men were obviously wrong. Once you commit to a relationship, however, the assumption is that you think the guy's okay, which means you have to start admitting that maybe, just maybe, you're less than perfect. This is new territory and you need to talk about it with your girlfriends.

That said, marriage and relationships can do strange things to people, and a lot of women I talked to say their friendships suffer when one of them gets married. That's because when your friends get married or enter into a serious relationship, it can feel a bit as if they've joined a secret cult from which you are excluded. I always liked the *Bridget Jones' Diary* reference to them as the "smugly marrieds." Suddenly, the two of them do everything as a couple and their minds seem to have been miraculously erased of any memory of what it was like to be single. And even though half of them have just as many problems as any of their single gal friends, they take pity on their single friends. You can become their pet project. "I know this reeeaally nice guy you should meet," they'll say. It's usually some guy she'd actually like to date herself if she were single, so instead she lives the experience vicariously by making you date him.

But even if your friend manages to avoid becoming a "smugly married," and manages to have a relationship and still keep her single gal friendships intact, it's hard to avoid the fact that her priorities are now different. "I'm in a serious relationship and it's hard to remain close to single pals who are still boy crazy," says Kate.

On the other hand, when you're a single person, it's hard to deal with the fact that your friend might not want to hit the bars and cruise men with you every Friday night. Even talking about boys can sometimes be less fun with a friend who's hitched, because, as I mentioned earlier, you've got less to commiserate about. It can be tough, too, when the single friends don't invite the hitched friends to stuff because they either assume she'll either be doing something with her significant other, or that because she's in a relationship, she no longer wants to go out and party.

For the single friends, they have to figure out how inclusive to be of the person's partner. Now when you invite her to something, you have to specify whether you'd like to see her with or without the partner appendage. Which can be particularly rough if you do not get along with your girl-friend's mate. "One friend is married to a man that doesn't like me and I don't like him, so I hardly ever visit her house," says Jennifer.

I've always struggled with this one. I realize not everyone has to become best buds, but in my rule book, if a guy is into us, then he should take a vested interest in getting to know and like our girlfriends, since they are such an important part of who we are. I have little tolerance for a guy who makes his girlfriend choose between him and her friends, and I have an even harder time with a friend who would date, or worse, marry, someone like that. It can really strain a friendship.

But I've seen it happen again and again. Sure, some women get uptight about him "going out with the boys," but a seemingly equal number of guys feel threatened by the bond women have with their girlfriends. Again, say Etaugh and Bridges, many men see their spouse as their best friend and sometimes get jealous and possessive when they think other close relationships—such as those his wife shares with her girlfriends—will threaten that primary bond. As if they know we share a Secret Language and hate that they can't crack the code. Poor boys.

Then there's the double-couple thing when couples start doing things only with other couples. "Although the couple-to-couple relationship is the most common friendship vehicle among married people, it is not without frustration," write Etaugh and Bridges. "Even if each partner in a marital pair had equal input in the formation of the foursome, the chances are that the eight relationships shared by four will not proceed smoothly. Often one pair of friends, usually the two who originally met, will enjoy the relationship the most, and the other two will attempt to be friendly in a forced way."

Which can really suck. While I've met some wonderful women who were the girlfriends and wives of friends of my various partners, I've suffered through a few couples' nights thinking to myself, Ugh, I'd so much rather be out with the girls.

Melody really felt this when she moved to Dallas with her fiancé. Her Tier One friends—ones she's known for fifteen years or more—were back home, and it seemed everyone she met in her new community was paired off and stuck to their significant others. "I love my fiancé to death," says Melody, "but I miss those girls' nights." Most of us, like Melody, realize that our partner is simply not going to fulfil all our needs. And despite social expectations or marital expectations, most women I know have worked hard to maintain the female friendships they had before they became part of a couple.

Margaret tells me about a book she read before getting married that was described as "the thinking woman's guide to getting hitched." The book described marriage as a rite of passage in which a woman transforms herself into a new identity. On the road to marriage, according to this book, a woman must sever ties from her parents, friends, and her old identity. "When I read this, I flipped," says Margaret. "I was getting married not because I wanted to be absorbed into my husband's personality or create some new collective entity with 'one soul, two bodies.' I liked my life, my friends, my husband, and I saw marriage as a step toward maintaining it all. The idea that a woman must give up her friends is bullshit."

Since tying the knot, Margaret says she's actually made more of an effort to keep in touch with female friends, whether it's a quick e-mail, a phone call, or brunch. For the record, while I am grateful to e-mail for having helped me maintain many a friendship, forwarded chain letters do not count as staying in touch!

Baby, It's You

Kids throw a whole new wrench into the works. I remember the first time I had lunch with the first of my close girlfriends who had a kid. I actually found myself annoyed that every time I launched into some no doubt earth-shattering problem I was having or tried to share some good gossip, the kid stole my friend's attention from me. I remember thinking, Oh no, while I still love her dearly and we remain deeply bonded, she now has two kids and I fear we'll never really have a decent conversation again. It's tough to maintain friendships with female friends when you don't have kids yourself.

"My sister is my best friend," says Susan. "Since she's become a mother, we no longer know everything about each others' life. She can't talk on the phone like we used to, and when I go to visit I spend my time playing with the children —visiting with her has become secondary." It works both ways. A woman I know said she found it hard to listen to her childless girlfriends whine and complain about their problems once she had a kid. Having a child had put things into perspective for her and shifted her priorities.

But that doesn't mean Mom doesn't want to have fun any more. "I resent some of my friends who I feel left my life when I had a kid," says thirty-four-year-old Mary-Anne, the mother of a one-year-old. "I still want to be included when my friends go out for a few glasses of wine once a week. They don't call me because they assume I won't be able to go anyway. Sometimes I can't, but I'd still like to be asked."

Things do change when you have kids admits Kirsten, a thirty-two-year-old mother of two. "You can't just drop everything and head out for the night with your friends when they call. You have to plan for things, and sometimes I feel like my friends don't get that," she says. "They don't understand how difficult it is just to have a good time. As long as you have your kids with you, you're working. And even when they're not with you, you're worrying about them." It's something non-moms have a difficult time grasping. Kirsten has two sisters-in-law her age who both have great careers and no children. "I can't even talk to them any more," she says. "They're not interested. And the insensitivity just makes me crazy."

It's difficult with friends who don't have kids, Kirsten says, because suddenly there is a huge part of your life that you are not really able to share with them. "Friends without kids will only put up with so much of you talking about your kids," says Kirsten, "But for new mothers, this often becomes the thing we want to talk about most."

"Before I was a mom, all my friends were career oriented, with no kids," says Darlene, twenty-eight. "I was the first one out of our group to have kids and all of a sudden, I felt like I didn't have any friends. It's not that they didn't call, but they weren't interested in anything I had to say because I couldn't talk about work. All I talked about were poopy diapers and throwing up."

Sometimes women without kids can be downright unsupportive. When Deann decided to stay home with her last baby, one woman actually made a sarcastic comment to her about how hard it must be to be a stay-at-home mom watching TV and eating all day. "I had another woman say she decided not to have kids because it ruins a woman's body," says Deann. "Then she looked me up and down and said, 'I guess you know exactly what I mean.' Can you believe it? Ugh!"

Child Support

Is it really any wonder then that moms seek out other moms? After all, when your body changes from a sexual, independent thing to a breast-feeding, diaper-changing machine, it's nice to know you're not the only one. "One of the things we get from other mothers is understanding and a sense of the common physical things we're going through," says Bev, mother of a one-year-old. "While my husband was always checking in to see that I was feeling okay and everything, when I really wanted to talk about what was going on in my head or how I was feeling physically or how my day was going, I'd call my sister, who had also just had a baby."

"You tend to seek out other people who are in your situation and create bonds with them," says Claire, a twenty-seven-year-old mother. "It feels bad to move on like that, but it's a survival thing."

After thirty-four-year-old Valerie had her first child, she had problems with blocked nipple ducts when she tried breast-feeding. She realized she couldn't call her mother for help because her mother came from a generation when most women didn't breast-feed. She ended up calling another mom, who talked her through the problem. "You need other moms who have been there to clue you in to this stuff," she tells me.

When Anne moved to a new city with a young child, she didn't know anyone. "We were struggling to stay afloat and here I was walking alone with this kid thinking, Oh my God, this is the rest of my life," she remembers. "I was out walking my baby one day, and I couldn't get the stroller through a shop door, and I thought I was going to die. It's ridiculous, but you are suddenly aware of all these things you take for granted. I didn't have a clue where to even find a fucking kindergarten for my kid. You need other women to help you.

I finally started meeting other moms. One mom told me about this deli that had extra-wide doors that fit a stroller easily. You'd think she'd given me the secret to eternal life, I was so grateful."

It's not always easy to find the support. Claire feels that in previous generations a woman's "support group" was built into the neighbourhood. Thirty or forty years ago, many mothers didn't work, so they stayed home, had kids, and relied on each other. "My mom used to talk on the phone every day—all her girlfriends lived on the cul-de-sac and there she'd be at the kitchen table talking for hours to her friend who lived across the street, while the kids played together," she says. "Now people move in, they move out. Or your neighbours might come in the back way, and you won't even know if they're home or not."

Kirsten remembers how tough it was when she quit work after having her daughter. "My first three months off were awful," she recalls. "I stayed inside every day and cried—I just hated it. I wanted to get back to work so badly. And then one day, I just picked myself up, went outside and started talking to people. Before I knew it, I had a whole new group of friends. I've heard the same story from a lot of women. It's a real shock to your system."

I saw what she meant when I attended a mothering group —a bunch of stay-at-home moms who gathered weekly in a church basement to offer support, companionship, information, and a chance to get out of the house. It was amazing. These women had an entire underground economy going on. They exchanged tips on where to get cheap kids' clothes. One woman spread the word that she was looking for a kids' toy kitchen set, another offered up a jogger stroller that she no longer needed, and one very popular woman said she had a line on some bargain baby wipes. All shared with coffee and delicious snacks, of course.

"You get validation," says Claire, explaining what the group does for her. "You think you're the only one going through all this, and then you sit down with other moms and find out their kids do the exact same things. You need to understand that what you're doing is the same as what millions of other women are doing, and that it's perfectly normal."

"You come in with a problem and you think it's all you," echoes Susan. "It's wonderful to have someone else say, 'Yeah, isn't that brutal?' or 'Don't worry, it's just a phase.' It makes it all easier to take."

"When you first meet another mom, you sit around the playground together watching your kids for hours and you talk," says Sarah, who is the mother of two kids. "You talk about your babies, and when you become better friends, you talk about your life and what you did before babies. Then you talk about your husbands, and then you talk about your babies again."

While this no doubt creates deep bonds—many which often last a lifetime—some women say it can also be hard when you suddenly realize that your entire identity is as your child's mother. "As your kids get older, and join soccer or whatever, you become friends with your kids friends' moms, rather than picking your own friends," continues Sarah. "Sometimes you feel like nobody knows who you are, except that you're so-and-so's mommy, and that's a little scary."

"I sometimes wonder what I'll be when my kids grow up and become independent," says Stephanie, who has two young children. "I keep thinking, What am I gonna do after? I'm going to have no skills, or What if my husband leaves me for his secretary?"

Men don't have the same fears, she says. They often don't get as emotionally involved in their children's lives. "My husband just wants the highlights," says Marie, laughing.

"Men just talk about their kids differently," says Stephanie. "My husband plays hockey with a close male friend who has kids and they do talk about things like diapers and how to get them into bed. But it's just not as detailed."

Father Doesn't Know Best

There are plenty of details about motherhood that elude Dad according to the moms I spoke to. "I think that for a lot of men, there's a 'window of relevance' when the baby is born because it's all so new," says Mary-Anne. "They're very emotional about it all, but they still don't deal with the child twenty-four hours a day, seven days a week.

At least he's better than he once was. According to a poll in *The Ladies' Room Reader: The Ultimate Women's Trivia Book* by Alicia Alvrez, young men are starting to put family before career, something women have done since, well, the first woman gave birth. Approximately 70 per cent of men in their twenties and thirties polled said they would be willing to trade pay for more family time compared with 26 per cent of older men.

Moms are still clocking in more time with the kids, though. While one in every three dads said they spend fewer than three hours a day with their kids, only one in twenty women spend that little time. But it's not just the kids that get less attention. In homes where both partners have full-time jobs outside the home, women still do 70 per cent of the housework. In 93 per cent of married households, women do the laundry, and three out of five women are in charge of the family finances. According to Statistics Canada, women and men in Canada have similar total workloads, but men spend most of their time, 4.5 hours a day, in paid work, and 2.7 hours in unpaid work. For women, the statistics are reversed, with 2.8 hours in paid work and 4.4 hours in unpaid work —such as housework and caregiving. No wonder one re-searcher, commenting on the overwork of most married women with kids, said, "These women talk about sleep the way a hungry person talks about food."

"I think it's just because a lot of men still assume it's the mother's role to get everything done," says Claire. "There is the rare husband out there who's more of a caretaker than the wife, but usually they rely on us to do it all." Unlike other women—even, surprisingly, women who have never been mothers—men often don't have a clue. "I wish he got the 'details' and really understood how much work it actually takes to get pull the simplest thing together," says Kirsten. "It would be nice not to be the only one responsible."

"I'm not sure they grasp how long and how much effort it takes to do certain things," says Susan. "Like whenever we go to the cottage, I find myself packing for myself, my husband, my eleven-year-old, my three-year-old, and my five-month-old. Now I just don't pack for my husband any more."

"You don't want to feel like a nag, so you don't say anything," adds Elizabeth, the mother of two boys. "But then you resent that he didn't do things on his own. I asked my husband to get the boys together for a family picnic. He got them a shirt and a pair of pants, and here I am whipping up the food but I have to stop and ask, 'Do you think they might need socks? Underwear?' Never mind a few diapers, a change of clothes and a drink."

Women learn this stuff through experience and by watching other moms, says Linda. "Like the one time we went out without the sippy cup we paid for it, and now we know not to go out without the darn sippy cup."

Taking a cue from her own lesson, she now lets her husband learn the same way. "I've decided to just let him deal with the consequences," she says. "I say, 'You're going out . . . you've got the diaper bag? Great.' I don't check the diaper bag. The only way he'll remember stuff without me nagging is if he doesn't have what he needs when he needs it. Next time, he'll probably remember."

In many ways, women create their own situations. On one hand we complain that men don't do enough, but then we give them a hard time when they try to do it and screw it up according to our standards. Often we just figure it's easier to take care of everything ourselves, and then we quietly (or, in some cases, not so quietly) seethe with resentment at the inequity of it all. Interestingly enough, in the poll in *Ladies' Room Reader*, single mothers were shown to spend less time on housework than married moms. So either men are making most of the mess or women feel more responsible when there's a man around. Considering that 53 per cent of working women said they were not willing to give up any of their housework responsibilities because they didn't like the way the men in their lives did them, I'm going with door number two.

It's not all our fault. We're taught to take care of others even if it means sacrificing our own sanity. After all, we've watched our own womenfolk—moms, grandmothers, aunts —do it for years. "My mom was so busy most of the time that when it came to the younger kids, I often felt like I was the mother," seventy-year-old Vera offers by way of explanation. "I helped make the meals, clean up, change diapers, bathe the kids. I'd come home at lunchtime and do loads of laundry alongside my mother. My sister Lois helped too. You just automatically did this stuff; Mom didn't have to ask us. You didn't usually see the guys doing much; they helped with the wood stove, sometimes, I guess."

We're also taught that while a man's home may be his castle, the state of his home is a direct reflection on us. "I wish I could leave my place a mess," says Sarah. "But there's still this implication that a messy home means you're a lousy mother and housekeeper. I can't let go of that."

Men are still overly praised for just pitching in. "I find I get angry when I thank my husband for doing some domestic chore," says Jody, a forty-one-year-old mother of two boys. "He never thanks me for all the things I do on a daily basis that he doesn't even realize I do. I'd like to be thanked too. Now when I thank him I tell him, 'I hope you realize I'm thanking you for something you should be doing anyway.'"

But it's tough on the boys. Some of them came from households where Mom did everything. And they just don't see that as an example the way women do, so, they're often clueless. "Don't ever live with a man who hasn't lived on his own," one woman told me.

While women have created support networks with other women to help us raise our children and to gripe about home life, guys don't really talk about domestic stuff with their guy friends. More often they get razzed for having to stay home with the kids instead of hanging out with the guys or they get flak if they're too domestic or "pussy-whipped." I still take notice when I see a man walking down the street pushing a stroller, or with a Snuggli strapped to his chest.

Even in this day and age, the only guy you ever see in ads for housecleaning products is the Man from Glad.

Group Outings

All of which explains why so many women need to get away from it all. Even family vacations aren't much of a break for Mom because, in most cases, she's the one who does the organizing, the packing, and the cooking. Sometimes it feels more like a job than a vacation, one woman said to me. You're not totally free. So women have to find that freedom elsewhere, and not surprisingly, it often comes from hanging out with other women sharing in our Secret Language.

"We had a twenty-five-year 'group night while we were all still raising our children and while we all still had husbands,' reunion," says Bridget, a fifty-year-old divorcée who was a stay-at-home mom until she went to work after her divorce. "We started with coffee every Wednesday evening, and gradually moved to wine and getting home at 3 A.M. We'd just talk and talk and talk. That got a lot of aggression out of our systems."

And just as men have traditionally had their boys' hunting and fishing weekends, women have started demanding their girls' weekends. The fact that more men are involved with child care (even if he forgets the sippy cup now and again) means Mom can get away and, as one woman put it, "just be responsible for me!"

Two of my sisters have institutionalized girls' weekends. When I showed up for the Friday night of one of these weekends, a woman was apologizing because she brought "lite" cream by accident. These weekends are not about restricting yourself. This is a time to indulge. And indulge they did. While much wine and food flowed (everyone brings food so no one has to cook), out came the karaoke and the outfits the women bring to play dress-up. The women laughed till they practically peed themselves and talked about everything under the sun, often loudly, and often over one another.

In the morning, nursing hangovers and coffee with real cream, the women talked to me about the importance of these weekends. Besides the escapism from their lives full of constant juggling and multi-tasking (not to be underestimated), one of the women described these weekends as a bit of an insurance policy. She knows if she invests this kind of quality time with her girlfriends, she'll be able to count on them when she needs them.

These women also give each other affirmation. Even as the hostess cooked up the eggs for the breakfast they had all chipped in for, the other women praised her perfectly turned eggs. No one compliments their eggs at home. They make one another feel appreciated and supported. They share strategies for how to deal with keeping it all together. They realize from talking that their kids aren't such horrors and that everyone else has the same problems.

My sister says she leaves these weekends rejuvenated— exhausted but rejuvenated. The added bonus is that after Dad and the kids spend a few days home without you, they have a whole new appreciation for you when you return. But you don't need entire weekends. Jocelyn and her friends have a potluck dinner on the last Monday of each month. It's a chance to catch up, bask in one anothers' strength and support, and laugh together. Its not just moms who need this, mind you. As we get older and life's changes threaten our girl network, we have to plan for special time away to reconnect.

Thirty-five-year-old Lana, a television producer, has instituted an annual retreat with three girlfriends. Although they live on different sides of the country, once a year these women get together for a weekend of heavy bonding, booze, nude sunbathing, and fun. "In ten years, through kids, marriages, divorces, and serious illness, we've never missed a year," says Lana. "We catch up on our lives. This is my inner circle, but sometimes life gets in the way and we can't always be there for each other the way we want to be. This is our chance to make up for that."

"We are one anothers' biggest fans," says Lana. "There is none of this 'Well, have you considered the other side' to our discussions. It's not that we avoid it; it's just that we truly believe in each other. We like being with ourselves and we know we've all been down similar roads. It's unconditional love."

It better be unconditional if you're checking out each other's labia with flashlights on the balcony. "Yeah, things get a little crazy sometimes," says Lana with a laugh. "I guess in some ways it's not that much different from a bunch of guys going away and banging their testosterone around for the weekend. But for women, I think it's got more to do with reconnecting. I feel like I plug into an estrogen battery pack." Lana says she gets strength and energy from these weekends that she can take back out into the world. "There is an amazing amount of love and support and it leaves me with a strong sense of who I am," she explains.

You don't always have to leave town or look at each other's genitals to sneak in some quality time with the girls. Book clubs are another way women get together. English professor Jenny Hartley researched book clubs in her book *Reading Groups*. Hartley says that while book clubs date back to the 1700s—when they were mostly male—they have now become a female phenomenon. This is in part thanks to Oprah. But the women Hartley spoke to gave her other reasons for belonging to reading groups: intimacy, friendship, support, a girls' night out, the opportunity to read different stuff, and a chance to stave off toddler-induced brain death.

Chris is part of a monthly book club. The night I attended with her, her husband joked that it was really an excuse to get together and drink wine. After he slunk off into the basement, it became clear that it was much more than that. This meeting was the first time the group had got together since taking a summer break. Before getting down to business, there was the usual fussing over new haircuts, catching up on the latest about their kids, and what they had done over the summer. One woman handed out flyers for a show of her children's line of clothes.

Ellen, the mother of three small children, says that though she adores the camaraderie of the group, for her the book club is the one time of the month she gets to challenge her mind. Reading books gives her something to talk about besides her kids. "Running after three kids all day, I sometimes feel brain-dead." It also forces her to take time for herself, something she says she has difficulty doing (never heard that one before). "I over-give all the time but with this, I can say to my kids, 'Sorry, no, Mommy has to read for her book club.'" As she tells me this, our hostess's young daughter comes into the room, wondering what she should do with her dirty soccer clothes. Apparently Dad, who is downstairs watching TV, is unable to answer this question.

Diane appreciates the opportunity to get together with a bunch of women every month and talk about something other than kids. "We were all people before we had kids, you know?" she says. And the bonus is that there is nothing intimidating about this group. "There is no feeling that you must be a superiorly intelligent person. I love that I can simply ask if I don't understand a word. I wouldn't be as comfortable doing that if I was in a group with men."

Thanks to the age range of the group—from late thirties to early fifties—the eight women also learn from each other. "When one woman talks about something she's going through and I've been there already, I can offer my experience," says Nancy, one of the more senior members of the group. "I've been there, done that, and it feels good to pass that along."

Although Allison, one of the younger members, came to the group to discuss books, she admits that the social aspect of the club is why she attends now. "When I told my mom

I was joining a book club, she said, 'You will know these women all your life. At the time, I didn't know what she was talking about. She's been in a bridge club for years, and they've supported each other through everything. Now, I sometimes think that with this book club the same thing could happen."

Women at Work

When a man gives his opinion, he's a man. When a woman gives her opinion, she's a bitch.

— BETTE DAVIS

While the Secret Language of Girls has survived centuries of private life, thriving in book clubs, through girls' weekends, and in other women-only spaces, what happens when we take the Secret Language out in public, like into the work environment? In a world where competition is expected and emotions are better left checked at the door, our need to feel connected and understood isn't always, well, understood. Often, female communication styles go against what is valued in what has traditionally been a male world.

Studies have shown that women tend to be less direct and confrontational at work. Men are more likely to interrupt and confidently state their opinions. Women are more likely to qualify their statements with a disclaimer like "This is just my opinion." As a result, women often talk about having their ideas and opinions dismissed or completely ignored by male colleagues.

Female colleagues, on the other hand, might ask why you hold a certain opinion, says thirty-three-year-old Michelle, who works in a company made up of mostly women. "This gives you the opportunity to really formulate your idea and come up with a much more grounded response," she says, "as opposed to being picked apart and having your opinions shut down, which is what I think often happens with men."

Women also tend to take things more personally at work. Twenty-six-year-old Eli, one of the only men in the company, noticed this as well. "I used to work in an all-male environment and I saw that when a man gets angry at work, he'll let it out in a ball of rage and then it will quickly dissipate," he says. "Women stew. They can dwell on a conflict for a week. They'll discuss it and debate it with whomever is willing to listen."

Jane, another colleague, agrees with Eli. "Just recently, I had an awkward conversation with one of the vps in the kitchen, and it stuck in my mind," she says. "I went over it— how should I have reacted? What does she think of me? Why did she say that?" We do the same thing in our relationships. We analyze—make that overanalyze—everything. Will he call me? Why didn't he call? What did he mean by that? What is he really thinking?

Eli says he's also struck by what the women in his office talk about. "I'd rarely discuss anything beyond work with the guys in the office," he tells me. "Here the women talk about everything—their personal lives, their relationships, their health, even their—I can't even say it—the 'p' word." You mean our periods, Eli.

But Eli admits that he finds the environment refreshing. "At first I thought it might be weird and intimidating, but now I love that I don't have to always be poker-faced at work," he says. "I can just be however I feel." Which is wonderful, unless, of course everyone is PMSing on the same day.

"Having an office full of women who feel free to express their emotions can make things pretty volatile sometimes," says Bridget, who is fifty and has worked for the same company as Eli for two years. "If we're having a bad day, we tend to paint an okay picture of ourselves in front of men. But with women, I think there's a feeling that we can let it out, be it crying or yelling at each other."

Jane admits it can be a little exhausting having to be constantly sensitive to everybody's feelings at work. At the same time, it's nice to know that whenever you have a personal problem that affects your work, you don't have to make excuses. You know the support is there.

Work Identified

No doubt, part of the reason women are less able or willing to separate work from their private and personal lives is that unlike men, we aren't conditioned to believe that our entire identity is wrapped up in who we are professionally. We tend to seek more of a balance between work, family, and friends.

The downside to this is that we often have to prove that we take our work seriously. Despite the fact that on average women in the U.S. now earn 40 per cent of family income, that one in six women earns more than her husband (compared with one in eighteen in 1968), and that 60 per cent of university graduates in Canada are women, we still assume that women are less serious about their careers than men.

Especially in fields dominated by men. Thirty-five-year-old Tiffany is a pilot for American Airlines. In an industry where women only represent about 6 per cent of all commercial airline pilots, she says that though it is assumed that male pilots are qualified for the job, female pilots often feel as if they have to prove themselves over and over again. Tiffany says that while attitudes have changed over the years and most people, especially other women, are supportive and say things like "'It's great to see women in the cockpit,' or 'It's great to have women in charge,' there's always some jerk that will climb on the airplane and will see me in the flight deck and say something like, 'Oh my God. There's a woman up there! Maybe we should change our flight.'"

As a female sports reporter, people often make assumptions about Kathryn. She says that while players are used to having women in the locker room, "a lot of guys think that I must be gay because I like sports. It's an automatic assumption—sports equals dyke. Why does one have to mean the other?"

Hazel, an attractive young female sportscaster at a cable sports network, finds that many people assume that sports fans are either male or unattractive females. She finds that she is held up to more rigid standards in her job. "There's a lot more pressure for younger women broadcasters," she says. "Men tend to take an ownership of sports. It's so near and dear to them, and they don't always want an 'outsider' filling them in."

For years, poet Kate Braid worked as a secretary, child-care worker, receptionist and a bunch of other "female" jobs. But she wasn't happy until she discovered construction in the late seventies when the small town she was living in needed labourers to help build a new school. She loved it and went on to work as a qualified carpenter for fifteen years. When there was no union work, she ran her own construction company—Sisters Construction. During that time she kept a journal and wrote several articles and essays on being a woman trade worker. When she left carpentry in 1991, she went on to become an award-winning author and poet.

"On every union job, and many of the non-union ones, I was the only woman and the first one the men had ever worked with," Braid recalls. "I remember one guy told me that he was opposed to me being on the job. 'Nothing personal,' he said, 'it's just that you're a woman.' At least he said it to my face. Most men didn't harass me—they were mostly confused and didn't know how to treat me."

Especially when the guys went for beers at a local strip club after work. "Going for a beer was part of the communication ritual," she remembers. "But because the beer joints were usually strip joints, I rarely went. Consequently, communication was difficult. I also noticed that [with the men], you never waited for compliments. I finally figured out that if they weren't yelling at me, I was doing the job just fine."

Eli noticed the different assumptions made about men and women when it comes to work when he switched from an all-male work environment to an all-female environment. When he first arrived, women in the office automatically assumed he knew what he was doing. "I think men walk into a workplace already at an advantage," says Eli. "They are raised to be confident, not to question themselves. Women tend to doubt themselves. They have to prove they are capable, but they are also judged on their personality and the way that they look."

Which makes some sense given how relatively little time women have been encouraged to have careers. In 1929, less than a century ago, fewer than 4 per cent of Canadian women worked outside the home compared with 55 per cent in 1999. And while women now make up just under half of the work force, we don't exactly have centuries of confidence backing us up. Plenty of us didn't even have mothers who worked.

Thirty-six-year old Jane had a stay-at-home mom who considered work to be the man's role. She was clueless about the working world. "My parents separated when I was fifteen, and it used to frustrate me because I'd come home from work and talk about my day and my mother would just say, 'Well, that's just the way it is,'" says Jane. "I still can't talk to her about my work frustrations."

Even for mothers who worked, like Bridget's mom, this was not her sole identity. "My father was a construction worker," says Bridget. "Our financial stability came from my mother's factory job, so it was almost a role reversal." Except, of course, that even though Mom worked, she still made all the meals and did all the housework.

In Michelle's case, both her parents worked and her dad did most of the cooking and shopping. Interestingly, the thirty-three-year-old has always felt closer to her father and finds most of her close friendships tend to be with men. But even still, she admits her parents never really took her ambitions seriously. "As a girl, I resented the limitations I felt being placed on me," she says. "I think that resentment has turned me into a bit of an overachiever and a perfectionist. It's as if I have something to prove."

Like Bridget's mom, women still straddle the domestic and professional worlds. Or if they pursue a professional career, it's sometimes at the expense of a family life. Not that all women want families, but men certainly don't have to choose one or the other. If they opt for both, it's not the same struggle as it is for women. Women have made far more gains in the professional world than men have made to the domestic world. In other words, if Mom and Dad both work, in most cases it is still usually women who handle the domestic side of things. Being caught between these two worlds can cause a bit of an identity crisis in some of us, strong female role models or not.

After staying home and raising her kids for thirteen years, Bridget says she had to go out and work for her own sanity. "I was becoming so narrow that I couldn't even make conversation in a mixed setting any more," she says. "It was always about the family or the house." But Bridget admits she has a hard time because she doesn't entirely identify with either role. "I don't define myself solely as a mother and nurturer, but I also don't feel like I have a strong sense of myself as a working woman."

Obviously there are women who are just as ambitious as men, just as there are men for whom family life takes priority over work. But on the whole, I think women—even women who do have a strong sense of themselves as working women —are still taught to place more value on other aspects of our lives. Even overachievers like Michelle. "I don't get my sense of who I am from my work and that's a conscious decision," she says. "Who I am and what I value comes out of my friendships and the things I'm involved in outside of work."

"Men often feel defined by their career, so their main focus is on success and getting ahead," says Lynn. "Women are used to having to juggle work, home, and social lives, so they often prioritize work differently."

"I work to live rather than live to work," says Jane. "I get my energy from my family, my home, my husband, and my friends—these are the things that matter to me. So if there's a problem at work, like if someone says something I don't agree with, I often don't fight back because it's not that important to me."

This of course goes against the male model of success, which is all about asserting yourself, getting ahead, and checking your personal life and your emotions at the door.

Powerful Language

I've been in situations with a male boss where I've been upset about something and had to fight back tears. Crying is seen as inappropriate, unprofessional behaviour, yet for me it's a natural expression of being upset. On the other hand, if a man is upset at work and yells at someone, it might be seen as inappropriate, but the man is not taken any less seriously.

In a work environment, women's style of communication is seen as less powerful. Even though, according to Deborah Tannen, author of *You Don't Understand*, in some cultures like Japan indirectness is the norm. In North America, when women are indirect it is seen as a weakness. "Ways of communicating associated with masculinity are also associated with leadership and authority," says Tannen. "But ways of talking that are considered feminine are not." Which is why, when a woman acts more like a man and asserts herself at work, she's often labelled a bitch.

And, truth be told, in some cases, some women do go overboard in taking on traditionally male qualities because that's what they we are led to believe we have to do to get ahead—"chicks with dicks," as my friends and I affectionately refer to them.

"I have had bad experiences with women bosses," says Suzanne. "They all seemed extremely paranoid about the ambitions of their female employees. And that's really sad because they should be mentoring us and encouraging us, not thinking of us as the enemy." It's tough. Women are still getting used to having power.

Although women have worked outside the home for years, before the sixties most women worked in traditionally female, non-competitive jobs. They were teachers, nurses, secretaries, waitresses, and sales clerks— nurturing and service-oriented work that called into play centuries of traditional female behaviour and communication styles. They were certainly not presidents, vice presidents, or board members. Even now, according to Canadian statistics, while women make up almost half of our doctors, dentists, and financial and business professionals, as of 1996, 70 per cent of working women were in teaching, nursing, and related health services, clerical, administrative, sales, and service occupations.

When women do yield power, it was and is often from behind the scenes—behind every man is a good woman, as the saying goes. Women who blatantly go after power are often envied by other women and resented by men. For women, wanting power is seen as selfish, and women are taught to be selfless—to be caring and to help others before going after what they want. So instead we often become martyrs at work, doing way too much, taking on everyone else's problems, all without demanding the recognition. Women are not taught to compete the way men are. We want everyone to get along, and competing goes against that.

Jennifer actually decided not to apply for a job because one of her female co-workers whom she considers a friend had applied for the same position. "I know this is a stupid reason not to go for a job," she says, "but I wanted to maintain our friendship. That was more important to me." As in female friendship, women are often unable to separate friendship and competition in the workplace. We learn that if we make our competitiveness obvious, other women will resent us. So, once again, we take it underground.

Sarah works in a medical records office at a hospital where she is largely surrounded by women. "Women talk behind someone's back to avoid problems rather than confront a person directly," she says.

"I like that men are more direct," says Krissandra. "Women skirt the issues too much because they are too afraid of hurting or offending someone. It drives me crazy. Just say what you need to say."

"Women tend to expect other women to read their minds," adds Amy. "They think that because you're a woman, you know the 'rules' of solidarity and co-operation, even if they're inefficient, and that you'll follow them. I don't follow them and female co-workers get mad."

Women are also still getting used to having female bosses. Just as Suzanne felt her female bosses sometimes acted out of fear of being replaced by women below her, female employees are sometimes envious of what their female bosses have. We're used to men having more than we do and having power over us. We're not used to women telling us what to do. We're used to women being in the same boat as we are, able to identify and empathize with each other's situation. So while a female boss can be a role model and source of inspiration, she can also inspire jealousy and envy in women who work for her.

Carol, a fifty-five-year-old office manager, sees this among the women she works with. "The women are always gossiping about other women in the office," she says. "They make up stories about certain people, and they're jealous of what others have."

After spending so much time in a male-dominated work environment, Kate Braid welcomed the one female boss she did have. "Having a female boss was a huge relief," she says. "We understood each other, how we worked, and what we valued," says Braid. "We spoke the same language. It didn't feel competitive, or like I was being tested. She was careful to explain things fully, making sure everyone got what she was saying, and was genuinely pleased when something was successfully accomplished."

CAR TALK

Sandy Spicer started NIC's Garage in Vancouver because she got tired of feeling intimidated every time she took her car to the garage. "When a woman shows up at a garage, they're looked down upon," says Spicer, a single mom who went back to university, got her Bachelor of Commerce degree and opened NIC's Garage five years ago. "It's like, oh yeah, you don't know what you're talking about."

But the truth is, while a lot of women may not know a gasket from a carburetor, most women do want to understand what's going on with their car. Spicer simply explains it to them in their own language.

"When I tell somebody that their fuel injectors are clogged, I'll say, 'You know how when you spray hairspray, it's a fine mist? It's not supposed to come out in globs? That's what's happening here.' And it totally makes sense to them." I dunno, when I do use hairspray (though we prefer to call it styling mist now, thank you very much), it's usually clogged and I can't figure out how to get the stupid stuff to come out properly either, but I get what she means.

As another example, Spicer will use the analogy that a car is designed like our bodies, with different parts performing different functions. "I tell them that an axle joint is like your wrist joint and the boot that goes over it is like skin. It protects it and keeps out grease and dirt."

NIC's, which was named after her father Nick and her daughter Nicole and stands for Non-Intimidating Car service, encourages her clients to ask a lot of questions and offers them choices based on their means.

"A lot of single mothers don't have the money to fix something properly, but sometimes there are choices in terms of what they can do," says Spicer. "A young woman came in the other day with an old car with over 300,000 kilometres on it. She doesn't want to fix it right. She just wants to fix it so her windshield wipers work! So I gave her about three different choices and let her choose. She said to me, 'You know, this is so great . . . because I'm in control.' And I said, 'Well, you should be, because this is your car.'"

Traditionally, women aren't encouraged to take interest in their cars. But NIC's is doing its bit to change that. Spicer tells me that recently her daughter was in her boyfriend's car when she said, "Oh my God, your rotors are warped!' And he was like, 'What?'"

A Woman's Touch

Some say that women's communication style is actually more suited to today's information-based economy. In *The First*

Sex, anthropologist Helen Fisher says the job market is changing in many ways that favour women's communication skills. "Women have communication skills, and here we are in the information age," she says. "We're seeing an explosion in legal mediation and arbitration, and women are really skilled negotiators. We're moving into holistic medicine, which views the patient in this very broad perspective; just what women are so good at. And we've got this huge world-wide aging population, and women are natural nurturers."

Business is moving toward "systems thinking" says Fisher, and that requires a more holistic, contextual approach, which is much more suited to women's style of "web thinking." Apparently, the part of the human brain that controls our ability to multi-task—the prefrontal cortex—is larger and more strongly connected in women. Fisher argues that women have the ability to see the big picture, are better at long-range planning, can intuit more from verbal cues and body language, and will consider more points of view. Men, she says, are "step thinkers" who compartmentalize their attention, focusing on just one thing at a time while tuning out extraneous details. This works well on an assembly line, says Fisher, but "with the growing complexity of the global marketplace, companies will need executives that can assimilate a range of data, embrace ambiguity, and set business objectives within a broader social context." In other words, women executives.

"The economy is actually changing in ways that are pulling women in," writes Fisher. "With the decline of the smokestack industries, you need an education and women are better at going to school, they're better at sitting, they're better at listening and they're better at talking."

In an article by Colette Bouchez for the online *Health-ScoutNews Reporter*, a recent study concludes that "women climb the power tree differently than men, but they reach the top just the same." The study found that men establish dominance from the moment they enter a situation, but women move more slowly, forming alliances that ultimately help them achieve their power.

The study was conducted at Northeastern University in Boston and involved fifty-eight men and fifty-eight women, divided into single-gender groups of four or five. The groups met twice, one week apart, to discuss problems related to raising children. The meetings were videotaped and the participants were interviewed privately after each meeting and asked a series of questions about the group, including whom they thought spoke the most and who was the most knowledgeable.

What they found was that during the first meeting of the all-male groups, a leader emerged right away, and the other men fell into a kind of power hierarchy that carried over into the next week's meeting. In the all-female groups, a different power structure emerged. "During the first meeting, there was no clear-cut leader," study author Marianne Schmid Mast says in the article. "Unlike in the male groups, in the female groups the power was distributed evenly among all the participants. They each spoke about the same and they interrupted each other about the same." By the second meeting, once the women were more familiar with each other and alliances had formed, leaders emerged in each of the groups of women. "What we realized was that women do assume power positions as easily as men, just not as quickly," says Mast.

Traditionally, say the researchers, men are thought to be more dominant. They have a more obvious take-control attitude, while women tend to be more laid-back and not so concerned with controlling everything right from the start, allowing for a more even exchange of ideas among all participants in the group. But "stop and think first" can sometimes be more beneficial because it allows the woman to not only know and understand those around her better, but also assists her in forming alliances that are likely to help her assume her leadership role.

What's more, Mast adds, it has been traditionally thought that because women approach power so differently, they can't feel comfortable in a traditional hierarchical system. So many women have been blocked from the uppermost reaches of corporate America; however, this latest research found that while women do wait longer to assume a position of power, they make strong alliances along the way. So when they do take the leadership role, they can be just as dominant and forceful as any men in the group.

"A woman boss considering a merger, for example, may be concerned over how the move will affect the individuals in a company, how many jobs may be lost, or how many people may suffer," Mast continues. "These are things that men traditionally don't consider when making a decision."

GLOBAL LEADERS

According to the 2000 Avon Global Women's Survey, which polled thirty thousand women in thirty-three countries around the world, women perceive female leaders to be more organized (67 per cent), communicative (65 per cent), creative (62 per cent) and people-oriented (54 per cent) than male leaders. Conversely, women consider themselves less likely to take risks, be aggressive, and be egotistical than male leaders. In Latin/South/Central America, however, women perceive their female leaders to be more aggressive and risk-taking than men.

According to *Megatrends for Women* authors Patricia Aburdene and John Naisbitt, as early as the eighties, business management consultants began to teach male managers to relinquish the traditional "command and control" approach to management. Again, for women this came naturally. In fact, say the authors, early descriptions of the "manager of the future" listed many of the qualities that women were already bringing to the workplace: more openness, trust, compassion, and understanding.

"Many of the attributes for which women's leadership is praised are rooted in women's socialized roles," write the authors. "The traditional female value of caring for others —balanced with sufficient objectivity—is the basis of the management skill of supporting and encouraging people and bringing out there best."

Hey, if you want to see a good manager at work, look at any working mother.

Long-Term Investment

This is when the Secret Language of Girls really pays off. Despite it being dismissed, ridiculed, or just plain ignored, all that time spent talking to your girlfriends, being there for each other, taking time to understand and be understood was not just a blast, it was time well invested. Because later in life, when the relationships have ended, or spouses have passed away, kids have left the nest, and work is winding down or over, you still have your girls. And bonus, you also have more time to enjoy them.

From 1948 through to the early 1950s, sisters Vera and Lois worked together on the assembly line at a tobacco processing/cigarette manufacturing plant. Most of the employees were female, including floor supervisors and forepersons, save the heavy-machinery operators and a few male scientists. "We used to sing and dance on the line," Vera, now seventy, recalls. "There we'd all be in pincurls—we were setting our hair to go out in the evenings—singing along to the music they piped in. It was a great old time working together with a bunch of the girls, until the bosses came in and gave us shit."

That kind of socializing pretty much ended for Vera when she got married and started a family. But she's found that as she gets older, she is reconnecting with some of her old friends. "After my mother died, I heard from an old friend I haven't talked to in over fifty years," says Vera. "She'd seen the announcement in the paper and said she'd been trying to track me down for years but didn't know where to find me because we kept moving. We spent time chatting about the old times and caught up about each other's family—and we're hoping to meet for coffee so we can catch up some more in person."

Vera says her sister-in-law has been meeting for luncheons and outings with "the girls from work" once a month for at least forty-five years. "Some of the girls are gone now, and some have lost their husbands, but they still get together to chat."

According to statistics, women live a full five years longer than men—the average lifespan for women is 81.4 years compared with 75.7 for men. Not only do we live longer, but we're also more often single than men later in life. Statistics also show that men are more likely to remarry following a widowhood or divorce. Among those aged seventy-five and older, only 30 per cent of women are married compared with 69 per cent of men.

No doubt part of the reason for this is that men don't have the kind of support networks that women create. Researchers find that women tend to have more intimate female friendships to draw upon later in life. For most elderly men, their spouses are their only close friends. Women are less emotionally dependent on their marital relationship. It's still difficult for women after losing a spouse, especially if you haven't managed to hang on to a few original Tier One friendships from before marriage. Don't say I didn't warn you.

"When you're divorced, a lot of your friends drop you," says fifty-two-year-old Maria, whose twenty-year marriage split up nine years ago. "You don't fit into dinner parties or dances or other couple activities. And if you stayed at home to raise your kids like I did, it's tough to start a new life on your own and to make new friends outside of your marriage." For women who have learned to rely on other women at difficult times in their life, this can be quite a kick in the stomach.

"When I broke up with my long-time boyfriend it was like a divorce," says Susan. "So many of my girlfriends took sides, mostly with him, even though they had encouraged me to break up with him because he and I were obviously no longer happy. That experience made me quite bitter about female relationships in general."

But most women realize that they need women friends, especially as they get older. "Older women are more likely to have a female friend who steps in when she needs help," says

Dr. Loretta Pecchioni, an assistant professor at the University of Oklahoma. She's done extensive research on elderly women and their relationships. "It's something we've done all our lives. It's part of our conditioning as caregivers. We're more willing to step in and take on the emotional burden."

Pecchioni relates her own experience of getting divorced. "My mom and I talked about it," she recalls. "My dad came over and painted the house. That was his way of showing me that he loved me. Fathers and sons go to football games together to feel close or mend their relationship. They don't need to talk about it; women need to talk."

But even if we still have a male partner to turn to, many older women still simply prefer to talk things out with a girl-friend. "We know we can't do it alone and we don't want to do it alone," says Pecchioni. "Women value having someone in our lives willing to be there and help. Men value independence. They are trained to be rugged individuals. They have a harder time asking for help." In the same way that men won't ask for directions, many don't ask for emotional help either. Women have no qualms about this. We expect it of each other.

With older female friendships, you also have a history, adds Pecchioni. "You've been through lots together and you develop an implicit understanding and trust. You fill in each other's blanks, finish each other's sentences."

"When I was ill recently, I asked a dear old friend to come and stay with me for the night because I was really afraid— I even offered to pay her for the inconvenience," Vera tells me. She told me, 'We've been friends for so long, you know me better than that. All you have to do is ask.'"

Women also tend to value quality over quantity in friendships as they get older, says Pecchioni. "They don't need a large network and tend to put time into the important friendships rather than those that suck the life out of them," she says.

Sixty-year-old Lorraine and her seventy-something neighbour Marg have been treating themselves to daily walks and girl-gab sessions for nearly twenty years. What started as a way of getting fresh air and exercise has evolved into an important and lasting friendship. "There's such a bond between us," says Lorraine. "We've come to the conclusion that we spend more time these days in Tim Hortons having a coffee and a chat than we do actually walking!

"The other day, for example, we were just talking about nostalgia and I broke down right there in the coffee shop," says Lorraine. "And Marg said, 'It's okay, you're still grieving [the death of your mother],' and that was a comfort to me— that she understood what I was going through immediately, and that she was there to listen. Or like when she lost her best friend. We'd been out walking, when suddenly she stopped. I hadn't noticed at first, but we were in front of a florist's shop. She asked me if I'd help her pick out an arrangement for her friend's funeral. She just couldn't do it alone, and it felt good to know I could be there for her."

Lorraine also has a regular coffee date with her sixty-nine-year-old sister, Lois. They have met every Tuesday without fail (barring illness or vacations) for over thirty-five years. It started as an offer of emotional support and companionship when Lois lost her husband. The ritual is always the same, Lorraine says. Put the teapot and the biscuits out, pull up a chair, and start yakking. "If one of the other sisters drops by—or if one of our daughters are around—I just put out another teacup. Nothing changes—we just keep on talking." The funniest thing, Lorraine tells me, is that even after all this time, she still phones Lois on Tuesday mornings to make sure she's coming.

Fifty-five-year-old Sharon needs her close friends to talk through things. "It really helps us vent our frustrations," says Sharon. "We know we can say to each other, 'My husband's an asshole'—something we'd be too nice to say to anyone else and you know there is no judgment being made. They accept you and you accept them, no explanations required. With girlfriends I think you can tell personal things, things that you don't want to tell your family for fear of upsetting them or just things you're not proud of."

Lorraine agrees. While she enjoys her weekly "sister" time, she also has old friends she still makes a point of getting together with. "I don't even have to see them regularly and, still, when we talk, we pick right up where we left off," Lorraine explains of her old gang, friends whom she met in Grade 10. "I know these are people I can go to for support and help and for understanding. There are some things you just want to pass by a woman first, especially when it comes to getting advice to do with health. Good women friends can

MOM THROUGH THE YEARS

At age 4, we think "My mommy can do anything!"

By age 8, it's "My mom knows a lot! A whole lot!"

At 12: "My mother doesn't really know quite everything."

Age 14: "Naturally, Mother doesn't know that, either."

Age 16: "Mother? She's hopelessly old-fashioned."

Age 18: "That old woman? She's way out of date!"

Age 25: "Well, she might know a little bit about it."

Age 35: "Before we decide, let's get Mom's opinion."

Age 45: "Wonder what Mom would have thought about it?"

Age 65: "Wish I could talk it over with Mom."

– Source unknown.

be very reassuring when you've got a decision to make and can offer a more objective view than a sister would."

And as we have all our lives, as we get older, women need to talk to other women who are going through the same things. "I haven't really accepted that I'm aging," says sixty-four-year-old Darlene, "especially in terms of the changes to my body and the extra pounds. Menopause was difficult for me; I started at forty-seven, which is young. I used to watch my mother break into a sweat from her hot flashes, and I'd talked to my older sisters about it, so I knew what to expect, to some extent. We've all compared notes. At least you know someone's gone through the same things."

Old Hats

When Sue Ellen Cooper, a fifty-something woman from California, bought a red fedora for a friend's fiftieth birthday, she had no idea what she was about to unleash. Soon, all her friends got red hats for their fiftieth birthdays, along with a copy of Jenny Joseph's poem "The Warning," which begins with the lines, "When I am an old woman I shall wear purple dress, with a red hat which doesn't go and doesn't suit me."

Besides wearing a red hat and a purple dress, the old woman in Joseph's poem also threatens to spend her pension on brandy, gobble up free samples in shops, pick flowers out of other people's gardens, and basically run amuck. The sentiment struck a chord among Cooper's circle of friends, and they decided that once a month they would all go out for tea in their red hats and purple dresses.

It struck a chord with others as well. Word got out, and now the Red Hat Society has 750 chapters worldwide. A Red Hat Society Convention is being planned in 2002. Not bad for something that calls itself a dis-organization. The only rule in the Red Had Society is that there are no rules, says Cooper. Except the mandatory red hat and purple dress, of course. These women are tired of people telling them what to do.

In each chapter, the women are free to socialize any way they want—tea parties, shopping parties, theatre outings, whatever they decide—all in red hat and purple dress. The goal is to bring women over fifty together to have a good time.

Cooper says that older women are tired of being ignored. "We're getting older, but we're not dead," she says. "We don't like a lot of the perceptions of older women. Many of us have a lot of life left, a lot of energy left, and less responsibility as far as family goes. We've been so dutiful and we're not sorry, but, you know, it's recess now—we wanna play and we wanna play with our girlfriends!"

When I showed up at a gathering of the Red Hat Society in Toronto to find fifty older women in red hats and purple dresses, I had to admit they were pretty hard to ignore. I wouldn't want to run into this bunch in a dark alley. And they were certainly having a good time.

"I didn't bring my Depends," jokes Mary Dawn, who is laughing so hard she can hardly speak.

"I think women have more fun with women," says her friend Cindy, the source of Mary Dawn's state. "We let it all go and say everything, unlike men, who hold it all in."

"It's also wonderful to finally be at a point in our lives when we don't have to care what people think," Mary Dawn manages to add between fits of giggles.

Cooper, known as the Queen Bee in Red Hat circles, says one of the joys of getting older as a woman is that you can finally let go of the competition. "I don't know if it's still this bad," she tells me, "but from when I was in my teens—with the exception of my few best friends—we were always measuring ourselves against other women in terms of our appearance, our performance, how we do with men. Now, we're all getting older, so we don't look that great. We can't be bothered to compete any more, and what do you know, turns out all these other women are great!"

Cooper acknowledges that while the group is all about fun, she realizes that for a lot of older women, life gets tough and they need a connection to other women. For many, their world starts shrinking as family becomes less present and friends are lost. But because it's so hard to meet new women at this point in life, it can seem easier to just live like this, however lonely it may be. The Red Hat Society helps stop that from happening, says Cooper.

"Women have said things to me, like 'Bless you for starting this. I had just moved to this area and it's so hard to insinuate oneself into a new group of friends at this age. We no longer have kids or sports, but now I have eleven new best friends.'"

That's what drew Ruth out to the Red Hat Society. The sixty-five-year-old says her husband passed away last year, her kids have left the house, and she just retired, so she no longer has "the girls from work" to hang out with. The Red Hat Society introduced her to a whole new circle of women.

Another woman I spoke to said she spent her life following her husband around with his job and had to make new friends in every new town, so she doesn't have a circle of friends that stayed with her throughout her life.

Suzanne says her husband doesn't have the same interests as she does. "He's a homebody, and I want to go out. It's nice to get together with group of women where it's not about volunteering your time or taking your kids somewhere. This is just for us." Through the Red Hat Society, these women have found travel companions, golf partners, someone to go to the theatre or to the slot machines with. One woman offered members classes in clowning.

For Christine, her Red-Hatted friends have been life-savers. When she was diagnosed with breast cancer, the women from her chapter rallied around her big time.

"There's nothing quite like a support network of women," says Cooper. "Women give each other empathy. We've all lived different lives but we've had similar experiences, so there's a thread of continuity, even cross-culturally. There are just certain instances when a man is an other, and a woman is another you. There's a lot that doesn't need to be said. It's a little bit mystical. You know, men don't understand women, and I think that women can't always explain themselves."

Building Bridges

Rita, Ellen, Valerie, and Adrienne—all in their mid-to-late fifties—have been playing bridge together every week for over thirty years. It has helped them sustain their bond through decades of relationships, kids, and work. "I don't even think we liked bridge when we first got together," says Rita. "It was more of an excuse for a weekly night out when we all had little children around."

"If we hadn't scheduled it, it just wouldn't have happened," adds Valerie. "With kids, you never went out at night, and you only saw your neighbours, so it was nice to go out and see your other friends without the kids."

At that time, the women admit they spent much of the night talking about their kids. But over the years, talk has gone from diaper rash to divorce and everything in between. Sometimes they even talk about bridge.

"It's nice to know you're not the only one who's dealt with a certain situation," says Ellen.

"We also laugh a lot," says Adrienne. "Sometimes we drink too much wine. It's just very cathartic." In the early days, beer was the beverage of choice—out of the bottle, of course. "I still remember my husband coming in and one of us was smoking a cigar and another woman was smoking a pipe. It was pretty funny. It was our chance to cut loose."

And they all admit that while bridge nights used to last until two or three in the morning (these days, the girls are a little tamer and are usually home by eleven) there was definitely more talking than bridge playing.

"It became like a bit of a soap opera in my life," says Valerie. "If you missed a week, you could go back the following and pick up where you left off."

It's a way of staying connected. "Bridge night forces us to stay in contact with people that you otherwise wouldn't," says Rita. "It's like the 'bridge' between us."

Final Words

A bridge seems a wonderful metaphor for the Secret Language of Girls. The link we have with other women, the life experiences we share, the communication and unique language we develop together are like a bridge between us, one we know we can cross at any time in order to connect with each other.

I recently saw a short documentary on Inuit women in northern Canada. Two women were demonstrating the Inuit tradition of throat singing. The custom was started as a game that women played while the men went off hunting. Two women stand face-to-face, holding each other by the elbows. One woman starts with an animal sound and the other woman must repeat the sound. When the first woman changes the rhythm or the sound, the second woman must follow. Back and forth this goes, the women soon falling into rhythm with each other, their voices overlapping until they are entwined in an intense exchange of throaty animal sounds that sound like music. The first one to laugh loses the game.

To me this was the Secret Language of Girls in a nutshell. The lifelong communication women share is all about following each other's rhythm, echoing each other's thoughts and phrases, until one of you cracks up laughing. In this way too, the Secret Language of Girls is like music to my ears.

I think this post that I found on the Red Hat Society message board says it all: "Good times are even better when they're shared. A good long talk can cure almost anything. Everyone needs someone with whom to share their secrets. Listening is just as important as talking. An understanding friend is better than a therapist and is cheaper too! Laughter makes the world a happier place. Friends are like wine; they get better with age. Sometimes you just need a shoulder to cry on. Great minds think alike, especially when they are female! When it comes to 'bonding,' females do it better. You are never too old for slumber parties. It's important to make time to do 'girl things.' And calories don't count when you are having lunch with your girlfriends."

Now, go call a girlfriend and have lunch.

The Secret Language of Girls Glossary

"What we say."
And what we mean.

In Relationships

"We need to talk."
   a) I feel totally unconnected and we need to figure out a way to connect.
   b) We need to talk about something I have probably been thinking about and analyzing with my friends for weeks.
   c) You've been very, very bad and you need to either understand why the hell I'm so hurt and angry, or you need to not let the door hit your ass on the way out.

d) I'm tired of you. We need to talk about how I'm going to drop your boring self.

"What are you thinking?"

I really want to talk and your silence is maddening. I have to know what's going on in your head because if you don't tell me I will be left to make up all kinds of things that I think you might be thinking based on my own insecurities, anger, frustration, and past history and then we are going to get into a big fight, so you might as well just tell me what you're thinking.

"I think we need to talk about this more."

I'm going to continue on this path until you agree with me.

"You need to learn to communicate."

Just agree with me.

"It's nothing, really."

What may seem like meaningless, self-inflicted trauma to you will determine how nice I am to you for the next twenty-four hours, so you better ask me what's wrong and you better mean it, and you better listen.

"Go ahead" (with raised eyebrows).

I dare you.

"Go ahead" (with normal eyebrows).

I give up. Do what you want because I don't care.

"Sure, go ahead."

Go ahead and do whatever it is that you want to do but be prepared to suffer the consequences and don't say I didn't warn you.

Loud sigh

This is not actually a word but a verbal statement often very misunderstood by men. A loud sigh means she thinks you are an idiot at that moment and wonders why she is wasting her time standing here and arguing with you.

Soft sigh

Again, not a word, but a verbal statement. Soft sighs are one of the few things that some men actually understand. She is content. Your best bet is to not move or breathe and she will stay content.

"That's okay."

I need to think long and hard before paying you retributions for whatever it is that you have done.

"That's okay. I don't want anything for my birthday."

I haven't seen you trying to sneak in any packages. Don't you dare forget my birthday.

"Gee, thanks."

Thanks for finally "surprising" me for my birthday with a weekend away after I have been hinting for months about how I would so love a weekend away.

"Oh baby, thanks. That's amazing. You're the best."

Thanks for realizing that I would love a weekend away and surprising me with it without me having to plant the idea in your head.

"It's your decision."

You can decide whatever you like, but it should be obvious by now what I think the right answer is and if you haven't been able to figure that out well then, we've got bigger problems than I thought and I plan to make you aware of them.

"I'm not upset."

Of course I'm upset.

"I'm fine."

This one has several meanings:

a) I am definitely not fine. I may eventually be fine but first I have to be really pissed off and go meet my girl-friends and tell them how much you suck.

b) I'm not fine but I just don't feel safe enough to be open about my feelings, so please hold me, talk to me, and try and figure out what is wrong.

c) I'm fine. Why on earth do you keep pestering me. What have you done that you think I wouldn't be fine about?

d) I'm frustrated but feel that I shouldn't be, so I'm going to punish you and make you worry why I'm not fine.

e) If you have to ask, I'm not going to tell you.

f) I am not fine and instead of asking, you should take me to dinner and make me laugh until I am actually fine.

g) I'm just fine. I'll muddle through and probably be a better person for it at some point down the line, probably after a year or so of therapy and journaling and obsessing about it for a few thousand days.

h) Go away.

"Does this make me look fat?"

I am feeling gross because I am PMSing/have put on "winter" weight/just got some bad news that shattered my self-esteem/have a really important meeting to attend and all my clothes suck. As for the response to this question, we expect something along the lines of "you are the most beautiful, sexy woman in the world and you are not fat, and personally I think you would look better wearing nothing, but if you ask me that outfit looks amazing unless you don't feel comfortable in which case let me help you find something to wear."

"Does this look okay?"

While in the same family as "Does this make me look fat?" this is subtly different in that it is not necessarily tied to our entire self-worth and is instead merely an expression of uncertainty about our outfit and you are being used as a test subject. Respondents must tread carefully. While we do not want to leave the house looking like an idiot, a thumbs-down may be perceived as an affront to our decision-making abilities and judgment. A lukewarm, "It's okay" is worse and will result in making you both an hour later for whatever it is the outfit is being worn to as we try on the entire contents of our closet and end up wearing the first thing we tried on. That is, of course, if we don't end up in tears or buried under the huge pile of clothing that is now piled up on our bed and strewn about our bedroom. An honest assessment, couched in positivity and combined with suggestions, such as "Hmm . . . the pants are good, but maybe a different top" is ideal. Women know this.

"Was that the baby?"

I can't believe I have to ask. What would happen if I decided to sleep through the night and ignore the kid? How can you be so insensitive to what I have to go through as a new mother? Now, get your ass out of bed and deal with it.

"Are you asleep?"

Please wake up—I need to talk.

"Honey, did you finish cleaning the bathroom?"

You're kidding me, right? You don't actually think that this qualifies as clean, do you?

"Honey, can you please remember to lower the toilet seat?"

Hey, dipstick, you left the toilet seat up again and I don't care what you say about how it's just the same as me leaving the toilet seat down and you having to raise it every time when you pee because that does not result in me dipping my ass in cold toilet water at 2 A.M. when I stumble in to pee and you've left the toilet seat up again.

"I'm thinking of taking this job in another city, but I'll totally understand if you can't move with me."

I'm taking a job in another city and I'll understand, sort of, if you don't want to move with me, but part of my motivation is that I am too chicken to outright ask you how much I mean to you without sounding needy, so I need you to tell me that you love me and you'd follow me to the ends of the earth.

"Do you think she's pretty?"

You better say that she's not nearly as pretty as me or you can forget about sex tonight.

"Don't forget, we've got that party on Saturday?"

I have only reminded you seventeen times but somehow I know come Saturday at five o'clock when you've got your feet up on the coffee table and are settling in for a relaxing night of TV and I remind you that we have a party to go to you're going to freak out. No wonder you guys need instant replays in sports because you've obviously already forgotten what's happened.

"Why don't we stop and ask someone?"

We've been driving in circles for the last hour, and I'm going to jump out of this moving car if you don't stop and ask for directions because it is quite obviously not "just up ahead."

"Was there something you wanted to watch?"

Are you going to stop and see what's on any of those channels you're frantically flipping past because you're driving me nuts. Now give me the damn remote control before I whack you.

In the Dating Game

"I'm not attracted to you in 'that' way."

I'm not attracted to you.

"I think of you as a brother."

Unless you're into incest, this is obviously not going anywhere, and I'm trying to find a way to kindly tell you this.

"I don't date men I work with."

I have a vague policy about not dating people at work because it comes in really handy in situations like this when I'm not really interested in someone but don't want to reject them and make things awkward at the office, but hell, if I could get that hottie in the next department to go out with me, I'd break my policy and hopefully you won't find us making out in the copy room one day.

"It's not you, it's me."

It's you.

"I'm concentrating on my career."

Even something as boring and unfulfilling as my job is better than dating you.

"Let's be friends."

I'm too much of a wimp to make a clean break, and besides, I like your perspective on things and it might come in handy when I date other men and need a male take on things.

"I don't know what I want."

But you're obviously not it.

"I'm not really into dating anyone right now."

I'm not really into dating you right now.

"You're too nice."

I'd rather go out with a guy who is elusive and unpredictable because I have come to believe that being in a state of constant turmoil and anguish is exciting and makes me feel like love is exciting and wild, while a nice, stable guy terrifies me and makes me think I will automatically settle into a boring, predictable relationship and soon have bad hair and even worse footwear.

"I never give out my number. Why don't you give me your number instead."

I'm too nice to reject you outright, but if you were smart you would pick up on this and not give me your number because the chances of me using it are about as good as the chances of hell freezing over.

"Sure, you can have my number."

I am so conditioned to being nice to people that I can't say no even if I'm not interested and I'm going to have to screen my calls just to avoid talking to you again but it seems like the only way I'm gonna be able to get rid of you right now. If a can of Raid worked, I'd try that instead. Besides, it's not my real number.

"Please call me, I mean it."

Please call me, I mean it.

"Don't call me any more."

a) I'm really annoyed with you but I need to know you care enough to fight for me so you better call me as soon as you get home and talk through this with me.

b) I'm not interested and don't feel like screening my calls, so save both of us the trouble and don't call me any more.

During Sex

"Oh Yes! Right there."

Well, near there; I just want to get this over with.

"Size doesn't matter to me."

Okay, maybe a little bit. If I'm giving my girls the universal pinky signal tomorrow, I might be a little disappointed but as long as you know what you're doing and have learned to compensate in other ways, I couldn't care less if you had a dick at all.

"I don't need an orgasm every time."

I'm tired and you're trying way too hard and I am so turned off that it would take my industrial strength vibrator to get me off right now, but I don't feel like dealing with your insecurities about my hauling sex toys into bed when you aren't able to get me off, so let's call it a night and I'll just masturbate after you leave.

"That feels nice."

You are getting warmer, but don't let that make you think you are anywhere near the home stretch. This is only the beginning, and I'll need at least about ten minutes of "nice" (spread across various parts of my body, yes, beyond my breasts and crotch) before we get anywhere near "that feels good" which is another good fifteen minutes to a half hour from . . .

"Don't stop."

Whatever you are doing, do not stop. I'm sorry if you have a tongue/finger cramp, I am right on the edge and one small shift could put us right back at square one.

"No honey, I've never faked it."

I've faked it, maybe not with you (not that you would be able to tell), but we've all faked it at some point in our lives. Lucky for you, I realized it wasn't worth it when I saw I had to make the real thing live up to prior performances so that I didn't get caught.

"Not tonight."

I'm sorry, guy, but because you have perpetuated the idea that men are ready for sex anytime, you have made me the gatekeeper of sex. But truth be told, when I say this, it usually means I just require a slightly different seductive approach than you pressing your hard-on into my back when you spoon me.

"I'd love to give you a blow job."

As long as you let me control the rhythm and speed and don't start thrusting it down my throat, I do enjoy giving you head. It helps if you don't smell like an old sock too.

To Other Women

"Wanna come to the bathroom with me?"

Will you come to the bathroom with me so you can pass me toilet paper under the stall because I will once again pick the only stall that is out of toilet paper or the one with the door that doesn't shut and because the women's washrooms are inevitably 330 miles farther away than the men's and often down some dark hallway down creepy stairs and because I need you to help stave off boredom because women's bathrooms always have a lineup and I need to borrow your lipstick and gossip about everyone else we're with and update each other on how the evening is going and strategize about how things will unfold and to make sure you don't walk out with a trail of toilet paper stuck to your shoes!

"I'm totally PMSing."

I just had a huge fight with my cat, I started crying on the bus on the way over here, I've got my fat pants on and I'm so bloated that a guy gave up his seat because he thought I was pregnant and the bottle of Advil I bought yesterday is empty.

"Oh my God! I just spent $300 on a new dress."

Please help me appease my guilt by telling me how much I need this $300 dress and how it really is a great buy because I'll get tons of wear out of it and how every so often you have to splurge for something you really want.

"Will you come bathing suit shopping with me?"

No woman should be forced to endure the humiliation of trying on bathing suits alone and if you don't come with me I will end up slumped in the corner of some overlit change room buried in a mound of skimpy bits of fabric that barely cover my huge ass, which has gone completely doughy over the winter, never mind that a small family of birds could nest in the thatches of pubic hair bursting out the bottoms of the things or the fact that I could probably sand floors with the stubble on my legs.

"I hate cellulite!"

If God really is a woman, why isn't cellulite the sexiest thing in the world since practically every woman I know has it?

"You look great!" "Really? Thanks, it must be the lighting because I feel like shit."

I know you just told me I look great and I should graciously accept your compliment but in order to keep us on the same footing, I will deflect your compliment and compliment you back.

"He finally asked me out."

Remember I told you I ran into him at that club—you know, that one where they play really good music on Fridays but all the women dress like Britney Spears and the place reeks of hair gel? Oh yeah, did I tell you that so-and-so went last week and really loved it? She ended up meeting this totally cute guy and they went home together. No, she says she doesn't want anything serious. It was just a one-night thing. I'm not so sure. She's seems like she's trying to convince herself. She can be like that, don't you find? Acts all cool about it but then next thing you know she's hunting the guy down. Anyway, I was walking along Queen Street yesterday doing some shopping—oh my God, they were having an amazing sale at Mendocino and I got this totally great wraparound dress, super hot. Oh, it's a sort of a purply wine colour and it's that great clingy fabric but thick enough so it doesn't like hug every lump and dimple. Yeah, it looks amazing with those kick-ass new boots I got last month—you know, the ones I got on sale at Brown's. Anyway, I was walking along feeling smug with my new purchase and I ran into him on the street and he asked me if I wanted to go for coffee. Yeah, he looked amazing. He was wearing these great vintage gabardine pants with this great fifties style jacket—totally a good dresser. Yes, good shoes too, classic but just a little bit funky without being trendy. So we go to that coffee shop right by that great bookstore. We have to go there this weekend. I wanna get Sophie Kinsella's new book. I loved her last one. Have you finished it yet? Isn't it great? I love her whole take on women and shopping. It's hysterical and so true. So we go for coffee and he bought me a coffee. So sweet. We sat and talked for like two hours. He told me about his business—yeah, he runs his own graphic design company—and asked me how the book was going. He even asked to see what I'd bought and when I showed him he said he could imagine I would look totally hot in it. Major points. Do you think I should wear it to the book launch or is it too slutty? I wanna go for sexy, but not too sexy, you know? Anyway, after two hours, he's like, I guess I should get back to work and we made some jokes about being your own boss and setting your own rules and then he asked me if I'd like to have dinner! Can you believe it? I've only liked him for like a year and haven't had the nerve to talk to him. So yeah, we're going for dinner next Friday. What should I wear? I can't wear the dress because he's seen it and knows I just bought it. You've gotta help me pick out something to wear!

Bibliography

Aburdene, Patricia, and John Naisbitt. *Megatrends for Women*. New York: Villard Books, 1992.

Ackerman, Diane. *A Natural History of Love*. New York: Random House, 1994.

Alvarez, Alicia. *The Ladies' Room Reader: The Ultimate Women's Trivia Book*. Berkeley: Conari Press, 2000.

Apter, Terri, and Ruthellen Josselson. *Best Friends: The Pleasures and Perils of Girls' and Women's Friendships*. New York: Crown Publishers, 1998.

Baumgardner, Jennifer, and Amy Richards. *ManifestA: Young Women, Feminism, and the Future*. New York: Farrar, Straus and Giroux, 2000.

Beetham, Margaret. *A Magazine of Her Own?: Domesticity and Desire in the Women's Magazine, 1800–1914*. London and New York: Routledge, 1996.

Bouchez, Colette. "He Says, She Does." In *HealthScoutNews*, 22 January 2002.

Boxer, Sarah. "I Shop, Ergo I Am: The Mall as Society's Mirror." *New York Times*, 28 March 1998.

Brumberg, Joan Jacobs. *The Body Project: An Intimate History of American Girls*. New York: Random House, 1997.

Bunkers, Suzanne L. "Faithful Friends: Diaries and the Dynamics of Women's Friendships." In Ward and Mink, eds. *Communication and Women's Friendships: Parallels and Intersections in Literature and Life*. Bowling Green: Bowling Green State University Popular Press, 1993.

Cassell, Justine, and Henry Jenkins. *From Barbie to Mortal Kombat: Gender and Computer Games*. Cambridge, MIT Press, 1998.

Coates, Jennifer. *Women, Men and Language: A Sociolinguistic Account of Gender Differences in Language*. New York: Longman, 1993.

Coates, Jennifer, ed. *Language and Gender: A Reader*. Malden, MA: Blackwell, 1998.

Crnkovich, Mary, ed. *Gossip: A Spoken History of Women in the North*. Ottawa: Canadian Arctic Resources Committee, 1990.

Davis, Natalie Zemon, and Arlette Farge, eds. "Renaissance and Enlightenment Paradoxes." In vol. III of *A History of Women in the West*. Cambridge: The Belknap Press of Harvard University Press, 1993.

Dodd, Celia. *Conversations with Mothers and Daughters*. London: Macdonald Optima, 1990.

Douglas, Susan. In *Consuming Subjects: Women, Shopping and Business in the Eighteenth Century*. New York: Columbia University Press, 1997.

Duby, Georges. "Affidavits and Confessions." In Klapisch-Zuber, ed., *Silences of the Middles Ages*, vol. I–IV of *A History of Women in the West*. Cambridge: The Belkrap Press of Harvard University Press, 1993.

Eichenbaum, Louise, and Susie Orbach. *Between Women: Love, Envy, and Competition in Women's Friendships*. New York: Viking Penguin, 1987.

Elgin, Suzette. *Genderspeak: Men, Women, and the Gentle Art of Verbal Self-Defense*. New York: John Wiley & Sons, 1993.

Ergas, Yasmine. "Feminism of the 1970s." In Thébaud, ed. *Toward a Cultural Identity in the Twentieth Century*, vol. V of *A History of Women in the West*. Cambridge: The Belknap Press of Harvard University Press, 1993.

Etaugh, Claire A., and Judith S. Bridges. *The Psychology of Women: A Lifespan Perspective*. Boston: Allyn and Bacon, 2001.

Fillion, Kate. *Lip Service: The Truth about Women's Darker Side in Love, Sex and Friendship*. Toronto: HarperCollins, 1996.

Fisher, Helen E. *The First Sex: The Natural Talents of Women and How They Are Changing the World*. New York: Random House, 1999.

Friasse, Geneviève, and Michelle Perrot, eds. *Emerging Feminism from Revolution to World War*. Translated by Arthur Goldhammer, vol. IV of *A History of Women in the West*. Cambridge: The Belknap Press of Harvard University Press, 1993.

Frost, Liz. *Young Women and the Body: A Feminine Sociology*. New York: Palgrave, 2001.

Godineau, Dominique. "Daughters of Liberty and Revolutionary Citizens." In Friasse and Perrot, eds., *Emerging Feminism from Revolution to World War*, vol. IV of *A History of Women in the West*. Cambridge: The Belknap Press of Harvard University Press, 1993.

Gelbart, Nina Rattner. "Female Journalists." In Davis and Farge, eds. *Renaissance and Enlightenment Paradoxes*, vol. III of *A History of Women in the West*. Cambridge: The Belknap Press of Harvard University Press, 1993.

Goodman, Ellen, and Patricia O'Brien. *I Know Just What You Mean: The Power of Friendship in Women's Lives*. New York: Simon & Schuster, 2000.

Green, Penelope. "Mirror, Mirror: The Anthropologist of Dressing Rooms." *New York Times*, 2 May 1999.

Griffiths, Vivienne. *Adolescent Girls and Their Friends: A Feminist Ethnography*. Aldershot: Avebury, 1995.

Hartley, Jenny. *Reading Groups*. Oxford: Oxford University Press, 2001.

Holmes, Janet. *Language and Gender: A Reader*. Malden, MA: Blackwell, 1998.

Houppert, Karen. *The Curse: Confronting the Last Unmentionable Taboo: Menstruation*. New York: Farrar, Straus and Giroux, 1999.

Inness, Sherrie A., ed. *Delinquents and Debutantes: Twentieth-Century American Girls' Cultures*. New York: New York University Press, 1998.

Karp, Marcelle, and Debbie Stoller, eds. *The Bust Guide to the New Girl World Order*. New York: Penguin, 1999.

Kinsella, Sophie. *Confessions of a Shopaholic*. New York: Bantam Dell, 2001.

Klapisch-Zuber, Christiane, ed. *Silences of the Middle Ages*, vol. II of *A History of Women in the West*. Cambridge: The Belknap Press of Harvard University Press, 1993.

Kostash, Myrna. *No Kidding: Inside the World of Teenage Girls*. Toronto: McClelland & Stewart, 1987.

Kowalski-Wallace, Elizabeth. *Consuming Subjects: Women, Shopping and Business in the Eighteenth Century*. New York: Columbia University Press, 1997.

Kuczynski, Alex. "Ideas and Trends: Enough about Feminism. Should I Wear Lipstick?" *New York Times*, 28 March 1999.

Lehmann-Haupt, Rachel. "In Women's Groups, Back to 'Girl Talk.'" *New York Times*, 11 April 1999.

Levin, Jack, and Arnold Arluke. *Gossip: The Inside Scoop*. New York: Plenum Press, 1987.

Leyser, Henrietta. *Medieval Women: A Social History of Women in England 450–1500*. New York: St. Martin's Press, 1995.

Lochrie, Karma. *Covert Operations: The Medieval Uses of Secrecy*. Philadelphia: The University of Pennsylvania Press, 1999.

McCracken, Ellen. *Decoding Women's Magazines: From Mademoiselle to Ms.* London: Macmillan, 1993.

McFarland, Melanie. "Women and Shoes: A Love That's Felt in the Sole." *Seattle Times*, 19 April 2000.

Mulholland, Joan. "Patchwork: The Evolution of a Women's Genre," in *Journal of American Culture* 19, no. 4 (1996).

Okie, Susan. "Shoes That Hurt and the Women Who Love Them." *Washington Post*, 12 May 1998.

Orenstein, Peggy. *School Girls: Young Women, Self-Esteem, and the Confidence Gap*. New York: Anchor, 1999.

Paley, Vivian Gussin. *Boys and Girls: Superheroes in the Doll Corner*. Chicago: University of Chicago Press, 1986.

Bibliography

Peiss, Kathy. *Hope in a Jar: The Making of America's Beauty Culture.*
New York: Metropolitan Books, 1998.

Pipher, Mary. *Reviving Ophelia: Saving the Selves of Adolescent Girls.*
New York: Ballantine Books, 1994.

Pogrebin, Robin. "Adding Sweat and Muscle to a Familiar Formula."
New York Times, 21 September 1997.

Ragas, Megan Cohen, and Karen Kozlowski. *Read My Lips: A Cultural
History of Lipstick.* San Francisco: Chronicle Books, 1998.

Railla, Jean. "A Broom of One's Own." *Bust*, spring 2001.

Raoul, Valerie. "Women and Diaries: Gender and Genre." In *Mosaic*
22, no. 3 (summer 1989).

Régnier-Bohler, Danielle. "Literary and Mystical Voices." In Klapisch-
Zuber, ed., *Silences of the Middle Ages*, vol II of *A History of Women in
the West.* Cambridge: The Belknap Press of Harvard University
Press, 1993.

Scanlon, Jennifer. "Boys-R-Us: Board Games and the Socialization of
Young Adolescent Girls." In Inness, ed. *Delinquents and Debutantes.*

Schrum, Kelly. "'Teen Means Business: Teenage Girls' Culture and
Seventeen Magazine 1944–1950." In Inness, ed. *Delinquents and
Debutantes.*

Simons, Judy. *Diaries and Journals of Literary Women from Fanny
Burney to Virginia Woolf.* London: Macmillan, 1990.

Slatalla, Michelle. "Selling Woofers and Tweeters to the Saner Sex."
New York Times, 16 March 2000.

Sonnet, Martine. "A Daughter to Educate." In Davis and Farge, eds.,
Renaissance and Enlightenment Paradoxes, vol. III of *A History
of Women in the West.* Cambridge: The Belknap Press of Harvard University Press, 1993.

Spacks, Patricia Meyer. *Gossip.* New York: Knopf, 1985.

Spender, Dale. *Man-made Language.* 2nd ed. New York: Routledge
and Kegan Paul, 1985.

Tanenbaum, Leora. *Slut!: Growing Up Female with a Bad Reputation.*
New York: Seven Stories Press, 1999.

Tannen, Deborah. *You Just Don't Understand: Men and Women in Conversation.* 3d ed. New York: Quill, 2001.

Tebbutt, Melanie. *Women's Talk?: A Social History of "Gossip" in Working-Class Neighbourhoods, 1880–1960.* Aldershot, Eng.: Scholar Press, 1995.

Thébaud, Françoise, ed. *Toward a Cultural Identity in the Twentieth Century,* vol. V of *A History of Women in the West.* Cambridge: The Belknap Press of Harvard University Press, 1993.

Theriot, Nancy M. *Mothers and Daughters in Nineteenth-Century America: The Biosocial Construction of Feminity.* Lexington: University Press of Kentucky, 1995.

Thorne, Barrie. *Gender Play: Boys and Girls in School.* Buckingham: Open University Press, 1993.

Tracy, Laura. *The Secret Between Us: Competition among Women.* Toronto: Little, Brown, 1991.

Tuttle, Cameron. *The Bad Girl's Guide to the Open Road.* San Francisco: Chronicle, 1999.

Underhill, Paco. *Why We Buy: The Science of Shopping.* New York: Simon & Schuster, 1999.

Vienne, Véronique. "Read My Lipstick." *Read My Lips: A Cultural History of Lipstick.* San Francisco: Chronicle, 1998.

Warden, Tricia. "Wayward Warden's Wicked War against Womanhood." In *The Bust Guide to the New Girl World Order.* New York: Penguin, 1999.

Warner, Penny. *Slumber Parties: 25 Fun-Filled Party Themes.* Minnetonka: Meadowbrook Press, 2000.

Wiesner, Merry E. *Women and Gender in Early Modern Europe.* New York: Cambridge University Press, 1993.

Wolf, Naomi. *The Beauty Myth: How Images of Beauty are Used Against Women.* New York: Doubleday, 1991.